The *313* Exchange

Anthony St. John

Book design by Anthony St. John
Cover design by Anthony St. John

ISBN: 979-8-9954637-2-6

Follow Anthony on his social media outlets from:

https://linktr.ee/anthonystjohn

I would like to thank God, first and foremost for his continuously guidance and love through this journey we call life!

To my family and friends: Thank for endless support making me to be the person I am today. Through the good, the bad and the ugly moments, you all impacted my life to make me a better person!

To the reader of this book: Thank you for taking the time to purchase and reading my book. I appreciate each and every one of you!

Stay tune for other titles…

Prologue

The penthouse was silent, save for the rhythmic, mechanical hum of the central air and the faint, distant sirens of the city below. The air was thick with the scent of expensive silk, expensive perfume, and the musky, lingering heat of the night before. Julius slipped out from under the Egyptian cotton sheets, his movements fluid and silent as a ghost. He stood for a moment in his "birthday suit," his body a masterpiece of lean muscle and calculated grace. He walked to the mahogany sideboard, his bare feet sinking into the plush white rug, and poured a glass of mineral water. The crystal clinked softly—the only sound in the room.

He stood before the floor-to-ceiling window of the 18th-floor suite. Below, the city was waking up. From this height, the people were nothing but ants, scurrying toward their "normal" lives—gray suits, bus schedules, and lukewarm coffee. He sipped the water, the cold liquid stinging his throat. He felt like a god looking down on a colony, yet he felt a strange, hollow envy for their mundane routines.

He turned his gaze back to the bed. Her name was **Helena**, a woman whose wealth could buy nations but couldn't buy a single night of peace—until she met him. She lay there, the silk sheet draped precariously across her hip, her face softened by a deep, satisfied sleep. Julius remembered the night before.

He hadn't just touched her; he had dismantled her. He had taken her on a cosmic rollercoaster, a journey where the physical world dissolved into a blur of starlight and sensation. He had been her navigator through a nebula of pleasure, pushing her until her voice gave out and her mind went quiet. It was a performance—a masterpiece of intimacy that left him drained and her transformed.

He walked to the bathroom, placing the glass on the marble vanity with a decisive *thud.* He stepped into the shower, the scalding water hitting his skin, washing away the scent of her and the sweat of the "job." As he lathered himself with sandalwood soap, the reality of his choice settled in his chest. *I made the right decision,* he thought, watching the water swirl down the drain. This was the forbidden lifestyle—the secret current that ran beneath the "naked eye" of the public. It was dangerous, it was expletive, and it was the only way he could see to escape the suffocating gravity of his old life.

Dressing was a ritual. The crisp white shirt, the silk tie, the cufflinks that felt like tiny weights of gold. As he adjusted his collar, his phone buzzed on the table. He checked the screen: **Deposit Confirmed.** The amount was staggering—more than his father had made in six months. A cold, cynical satisfaction settled in his gut.

He walked back to the bed. Helena stirred slightly but didn't wake. He sat on the edge of the mattress, the weight of his suit a stark contrast to her nakedness. He reached out, his calloused thumb gently cresting the silk of her hair. He leaned down, pressing a soft, lingering kiss to her temple.

"Goodbye, Helena," he whispered, his voice a ghost of the passion he had feigned hours ago.

As he walked down the long, carpeted hallway toward the elevator, the heavy silence of the hotel began to peel back the layers of his composure. He thought back to that terrible rainy night a couple of months ago—the night that had broken him and led him to Dominic's door. The memory felt like a bruise he couldn't stop touching. The elevator doors slid open with a soft chime, the mirrored walls reflecting a man who looked like he belonged in the sunlight, even though he lived in the dark.

1

Early afternoon light filtered through Venetian blinds, casting thin stripes across his worn leather jacket. The ticking of the clock, in the small 2nd-floor office on W. Congress St., was louder than it had any right to be. It was a rhythmic, mechanical judgment that filled the silence between them.

Julius Sterling sat in the low-slung leather chair, his hands clasped tightly in his lap. He wasn't wearing the suit that day; he was wearing a plain sweater, trying to look like the "normal" twenty-four-year-old, 6'1, 190lbs person would look. But the way he scanned the room—noting the exits, the weight of the paperweight on the desk, the tension in the woman's shoulders—betrayed him.

Across from him, Dr. Alvarez adjusted her notebook and offered a steady, measured gaze. Her glasses perched on the tip of her nose. She didn't look like a socialite or a madam; she looked like the truth.

"Tell me about the hardest moment this week," she prompted, her voice soft but firm.

Julius inhaled, bracing for the familiar ache of confession. "I've been restless. It started as anxiety, then the hypersexual impulse took over," he swallowed, rubbing his hand over his forehead, his fingernails scratching against his brown skin. "I chased it in ways I hated. I ended up... using the internet to feed the need." His voice faltered, his gaze dropping to the floor. "I ended up feeling more alone. And the worst part was, Maya was right there. She was in the apartment, she was in the bed, but I couldn't reach for her."

He looked up at Dr. Alvarez, his eyes clouded with a mix of shame and frustration.

"It had been two months," he whispered, the number sounding like a death toll in the small office. "Two months since we'd even touched. I tried to initiate, I tried to find that spark, but Maya... she just wasn't there anymore. Every time I reached for her, she was 'too tired,' or she had a headache, or she just rolled over before I could even find the words." He rubbed his face, his soft palms rasping against his stubble.

"She was ignoring me, Dr. Alvarez. It was like she had built this wall of indifference, and I was standing on the other side, starving. I had this hypersexual drive screaming inside me—the 'performer' begging to be let out—and the one person who was supposed to be my safe harbor wouldn't even look at me that way. I was dying to be wanted by her, but instead, I was sitting in the dark with my laptop, feeding a need that only made me feel like a monster." He looked at the clock, the ticking feeling like a countdown.

Dr. Alvarez nodded. "We'll explore the triggers. Remember, identifying the urge is the first step to mastering it."

Julius leaned back, tension ringing through his shoulders. A memory flickered: scrolling late at night, chasing one rush to the next. Each search promised relief and delivered more emptiness.

"What were you feeling before you went to that website?" she asked.

He paused. "Empty. Like I'd just run a marathon in my head."

"That emptiness was a signal. Instead of filling the void with sex, what could you fill it with?"

Julius looked at the photo of a young girl standing in front of a spaceship, with an older man on one knee. His arm was around her waist as innocent smiles showered the moment. "I… I didn't know. Music? Exercise?"

"Let's try both. Next time the urge hit, you'll have two go-to options. We'll name them now."

"Song playlist and a ten-minute walk, gotcha, doc."

Dr. Alvarez smiled. "Perfect. You're building a toolbox." She opened her notebook to a page marked "Impulse Mapping" and drew two columns. The first column had the header "Triggers" with the words "boredom," "loneliness," and "fatigue" underneath. The second column had the header "Responses" with the words "scrolling," "anonymous chats," and "risky meetups" underneath.

"Fatigue. I was exhausted most of the time, but I pushed through the moment. After working, I craved a distraction," Julius admitted. His eyes flicked to the window, as if escape might appear there. He continued, "The fatigue was always brought on by the ongoing dissatisfaction of what my fibers yawned for, fulfilling my sexual appetite."

"Fatigue lowered our impulse control," Dr. Alvarez explained. "What if, instead of reaching for distraction, you honored that tiredness? Rest could have become an act of self-care rather than weakness."

Julius considered this. The idea of permission to rest felt foreign—like a lifeline tossed to someone drowning in their own expectations. Dr. Alvarez introduced a four-point strategy: Pause and label the urge ("Restlessness"), Breathe through the craving for three minutes, journal a quick reflection on the feeling, and choose a low-stimulation activity.

"I'll be lucky to last 30 seconds before thinking about what porn scene category to pick for my next rendezvous," Julius thought to himself.

"Let's role-play," she suggested.

Julius mimicked exasperation, his hands cutting through the air. "I feel restless. I want to—" He stopped abruptly and shook his head. "No. Pause. Breathe." He inhaled deeply, counted silently, and let the air out in a slow, controlled whistle.

Dr. Alvarez smiled. "Good. Now, what comes next?"

"Journal," he said, his voice quieter and steadier. "Write what I'm feeling before I act on it."

"Excellent. You're reclaiming control." Dr. Alvarez handed him a printed worksheet. "Commit to these steps this week. We'll review your progress next month."

A sharp vibration buzzed in Julius's pocket. He pulled out his phone. The screen displayed a message from an unknown number: *Seward St. Now. Don't make me wait.* Julius felt his pulse quicken, the calm of the room suddenly feeling very far away. He stared at the address for a beat too long before sliding the phone back into his pocket, forcing his focus back to the doctor to finish the session.

Julius looked down at the worksheet, the crisp white paper glaring under the office lights. He began to fold it with agonizing precision, matching the corners perfectly as though the document might unravel or shatter if handled too roughly. He stood up, his muscles still humming with a restless, coiled tension that even the breathing exercises couldn't quite reach.

"Thanks, Doc," he murmured, his voice sounding hollow to his own ears. "I'll try."

Dr. Alvarez leaned forward slightly, her gaze softening. The room was quiet, save for the rhythmic ticking of a small clock on her bookshelf. "You're making progress, Julius. But we've been dancing around the edges of the real pain." She paused, letting the silence settle between them. "Next time, I think it's time we really open up about your mother's passing. We need to look at that wound if we want it to heal."

Julius felt a sudden, sharp constriction in his throat, like a hand tightening around his windpipe. The mention of her name brought a flash of a hospital room—the smell of antiseptic and the sound of a fading heart monitor. He swallowed hard, forcing the memory back down into the dark.

"Maybe," he said, the word barely a whisper. He wasn't ready to go there, but he couldn't bring himself to say no.

"You're not trying alone," she offered, her smile small but anchored in a genuine, encouraging warmth.

Julius managed a tight, appreciative nod in return, though the weight in his chest felt twice as heavy as when he had walked in. He turned and stepped out of the office, the transition from the soft-lit room to the sterile hallway feeling like a slap. The fluorescent lights overhead hummed with a low, maddening buzz that vibrated in his skull.

As he walked toward the exit, he slid the folded worksheet into his back pocket. It felt like a flimsy shield against the world waiting for him outside. He checked his phone one last time, the address on Seward Street glowing on the screen, a cold reminder of the "tiresome" and dangerous day of work that was only just beginning.

He reached his car and drove toward the heart of the city, eventually pulling over on Seward Street, nestled between Linwood and Rosa Parks Boulevard. After killing the engine, he sat for a moment, looking around the neighborhood and checking his mirrors before stepping out.

Julius climbed the stairs, his boots thudding softly on the wood. He knocked. Silence stretched for several long moments until a muffled voice drifted through the wood.

"Who the fuck is it?"

"Jay" Julius replied, his voice low but firm. "Open up the damn door, mane."

The heavy mechanism of the lock clicked and turned. The door swung open slowly, revealing Thomas, AKA T-Boogie. Standing 6'4" with a solid, athletic build, the bald man loomed in the doorway wearing nothing but a black tank top and jogging pants. He didn't say a word, his presence filling the frame.

Julius stepped over the threshold into the dim, stale air of the foyer before Travis—known on these streets as T-Boogie—could even think about swinging the door shut. The house smelled of old wood, blunt wraps, and the faint, metallic tang of a space heater working too hard.

Before Julius could move toward the back, T-Boogie stepped into his path, his massive hands reaching out. He began a practiced, heavy-handed pat-down, his palms slapping against Julius's jacket and waistline with a rhythmic thud. Julius didn't flinch, though the intrusion made his jaw tighten. "You know I don't have any weapons on me, man," he muttered, his voice echoing in the narrow hallway.

T-Boogie stepped back, a slow, shark-like grin spreading across his face. "You right," he grunted, his deep voice vibrating in the small space. "Your face is enough to kill anybody."

Julius didn't miss a beat. He started walking away, tossing a casual glance over his shoulder. "That's cute. Hey, did you ever make it to the drugstore for that little... *problem* you've got going on down there?"

T-Boogie stopped mid-stride, his expression shifting from a smirk to genuine confusion. He looked down at himself, then back at Julius, his eyes shifting warily. "What? What problem?"

Julius let out a sharp, mocking bark of a laugh. "From Tiffany, man. She told me last night that your dick is smaller than a baby's pinky toe." He paused at the edge of the dining room, a wicked glint in his eye. "She told me that right after I took her to... **SPACE MOUNTAIN!**"

The tension in the hallway snapped into a roar of laughter. T-Boogie shook his head, a reluctant, booming chuckle erupting from his chest as he shoved Julius's shoulder.

Julius shook off the contact, still grinning, as he reached the dining room. The air here was thicker, clouded by a haze of blue cigarette smoke that swirled under a single, low-hanging light bulb. In the center of the room sat a scarred oak dining table, where four men were hunched over, their faces illuminated by the harsh light. The rhythmic *slap-slap-slap* of cards hitting the wood punctuated the low murmur of their voices. They were deep into a game of spades, their eyes flicking toward Julius with a mix of recognition and cold calculation.

Julius pulled up a mismatched wooden chair, the legs scraping harshly against the linoleum floor. The dining room felt smaller than it was, crowded by the presence of the four men huddled around the scarred table.

"Whatupdoe, fellas?" Julius asked, his voice steady as he scanned the faces.

"Hey, young fella," Eric Grant grunted without looking up, his eyes locked on the hand of cards he was fanning out. Beside him, Bill Ellis gave a short, respectful nod, his face partially obscured by the haze of smoke.

Across from them sat Joe Burton and Buddy "High-Roller" Douglass. Buddy was a legend in these streets and the casinos—the Robin Hood of the drug scene. He had built an empire by bleeding other pushers dry and funneling a fraction of the spoils back into the neighborhood, a move that bought him both undying loyalty from the community and a massive spike in his profit margins.

Joe Burton, the eldest of the group, squinted through the smoke. "You got a familiar face, kid," he rasped, his voice sounding like dry leaves skittering on pavement.

High-roller didn't miss a beat as he tossed a spade onto the table with a sharp *snap*. "That's Julius," Buddy said, his tone commanding. "John and Mary Sterling's boy."

The mention of the name caused Joe to pause. He reached up, adjusting his thick glasses as if a better view would unlock a vault of memories. "Mary Sterling..." Joe murmured, his brow furrowing. "Wait, didn't she pass away a couple months back?"

Joe's memory flickered and then cut out completely, like a television screen turning black when the electricity bill had passed its final notice. He trailed off, his mouth hanging slightly open as he lost the thread.

A sudden, suffocating silence dropped over the room. The hum of the refrigerator in the kitchen felt deafening. Julius felt a sharp pang in his chest, the "breathing techniques" from Dr. Alvarez's office feeling miles away. The grief he had been trying to journal away surged up, hot and heavy in his throat.

"Yeah," Julius finally said, his voice tight but clear. "She left us a couple of months ago."

The air in the room grew thick with an awkward, heavy emotion that these men weren't equipped to handle. Sensing the mood soured, Buddy moved with a sharp, practiced efficiency to cut through the tension. He reached under the table, his gold watch glinting under the low light, and hauled up a small, weathered gym bag. A bright yellow handle was stitched into the side, standing out like a warning sign against the dark fabric.

He slammed the bag onto the table, the heavy *thud* scattering a few loose cards and silencing any further talk of the dead. High-Roller leaned forward, his jewelry catching the dim light as he slid the gym bag across the scarred wood toward Julius.

"Take this to Lenny at Club Connect on Chene," Buddy commanded, his voice dropping into a professional register that signaled the end of the small talk.

Julius gripped the yellow handle, the weight of the bag solid and cold. "Chene... Got it."

He went to pull the bag away, but Buddy didn't let go. His hand remained clamped on the strap, his eyes locking onto Julius's with a sudden, piercing gravity. "You've been doing a fine job, Julius. But we both know this arrangement is getting close to the end."

Julius felt a strange flutter in his chest—a mixture of terrifying uncertainty and soaring relief. This hustle had been his lifeline, the only way he could afford to bury his mother with the dignity she deserved, right next to the love of her life.

"What are you saving for now?" Buddy asked, his tone softening just a fraction.

"Paying my student loans, bills, redoing my parent's crypt plaque, and a wedding ring." Julius said, his voice thick with the memory of the worksheet in his pocket. "For both of them. Together."

Buddy nodded slowly, a rare look of genuine respect crossing his weathered face. "That's honorable. I've watched you and your sister; you both turned out to be good kids. That's why once you hit that goal, we're done. Your heart is too pure for this, Julius. You weren't built for the gutter."

Julius felt his pride flare up, a defensive heat rising in his neck. "You know I can take care of myself. I was in ROTC for two years, man."

The table erupted. Buddy let out a booming chuckle that rattled the light fixture. "I know! And you got kicked out because you tried to fight the whole damn platoon at once! You're one tough cookie, kid, but you still got a heart. I need ice-cold blood on my team. Now get out of here—you're breaking my concentration. I've got books to win."

Julius checked his watch, the hands ticking toward the start of his shift at his legitimate job. He had to move fast. He stood up, slinging the bag over his shoulder, but couldn't resist one last look at the game. He leaned over Joe's shoulder, squinting at the cards played in the old man's hand.

"Yo, Joc," Julius whispered with a smirk. "You reneged on that last book."

Joe froze, pulling his cards closer to his face as Eric flipped over the last set on the table. The realization hit Joe like a physical blow. He slammed his remaining cards onto the wood with a deafening *smack*. "DAMN!"

"That's it!" Eric barked, throwing his hands up in frustration. "This is the last time this blind muthafucka is my partner! I'm done!"

"Fuck you, muthafucka!" Joe yelled back, his voice cracking with age and irritation.

Julius laughed, the sound feeling good in his lungs as he headed for the door. The grief and the stress were still there, but for a moment, the chaos of the room felt like home.

T-Boogie was waiting by the door, pulling it opens with a mocking grin. "Get out of here, you ugly nigga," he grunted.

Julius stepped out onto the porch, the cool air hitting his face. He looked back over his shoulder, his eyes glinting with mischief. "See you later, little dick!"

He didn't wait for the roar of T-Boogie's response. He jogged down the stairs toward his car, the gym bag heavy against his hip. As he climbed into the driver's seat, a sudden wave of melancholy washed over him. Soon, the burials would be done. The plaques would be set. And this world—the only thing keeping him afloat since his mother died—would be closed to him forever. He felt like a man standing on a bridge that was burning at both ends, wondering what kind of person he would be when he finally reached the other side.

The drive to Chene Street felt like a bridge between two worlds. As Julius maneuvered through the mid-morning traffic, the gym bag sat on the passenger seat like a silent passenger, its weight a physical reminder of the life he was trying to outrun. He kept thinking about Dr. Alvarez's worksheet in his back pocket and the "Space Mountain" joke he'd just cracked at T-Boogie's. The contrast was enough to give him whiplash—one minute he was practicing mindfulness, and the next he was a courier for the city's most benevolent kingpin.

He pulled up to Club Connect. In the daylight, the building looked exhausted. The neon signs were dark, and the brickwork was stained by decades of city soot, but the place still hummed with a low-frequency power. This was where the night lived, even when the sun was high.

Julius killed the engine and sat for a second. The thought of his mother hit him again—the way she used to hum while she cooked, a sound that was the polar opposite of the heavy bass that usually shook this block. He was so close to finishing the crypt. So close to giving her and his father the permanent, beautiful resting place they deserved. But the thought of the "arrangement" ending left a cold pit in his stomach. Without the hustle, who was he? Just another guy working a tiresome shift, mourning a woman he couldn't bring back.

He grabbed the yellow handle of the bag, checked his mirrors, and stepped out.

The side door of Club Connect groaned as Julius stepped inside, but the usual midday stillness had been replaced by a whirlwind of electric energy. The venue was waking up for a massive event, the air thick with the scent of floor wax, expensive cologne, and the ozone of freshly tested fog machines. Technicians moved like shadows across the stage, and sudden bursts of violet and strobe-gold light slashed through the dim room, reflecting off the mirrored walls like silent lightning.

Near the main part of the bar, he spotted a familiar face. Leon Moore, one of the bartenders, was busy hauling a crate of premium liquor, his brow slick with sweat.

"Long time no see, bruh," Leon said, wiping his hands on a rag as he stepped toward Julius with a weary but genuine grin.

"Yeah," Julius replied, adjusting the weight of the gym bag on his shoulder. "I've been handling some business, man. Staying busy."

Leon's expression shifted, the professional hustle softening into something more personal. "I heard about your mom, Jay. Condolence to your loss. She was a queen."

The mention of his mother sent a sharp, cold ripple through Julius's chest, threatening to break the composure he'd worked on with Dr. Alvarez. He swallowed the lump in his throat and gave a stiff, appreciative nod. "Thanks, mane. I appreciate that." He quickly pivoted, his eyes scanning the chaotic room to keep the grief at bay. "So, what's the move? The vibe in here is crazy."

"Theme is 'Midnight Royalty,'" Leon said, gesturing to the velvet drapes being hoisted toward the ceiling. "It's gonna be a movie. You coming out to catch the vibe?"

Julius felt the pull of the lights and the music, the desire to lose himself in a crowd where no one knew his name or his pain. But he thought of his shift and the worksheet in his pocket. "Not tonight. I'm back on the plantation tonight," he said with a dry, tired chuckle. "But next time fo' sho." He patted the gym bag significantly. "Where's Lenny at?"

"He was just walking around here a minute ago," Leon said, glancing toward the back. "Maybe he went back to the office to check the books."

"Bet. I'll holla at you later!" Julius said. He reached out, and the two men exchanged a quick, firm dap—the slap of their palms echoing against the mahogany bar.

Julius turned away, heading toward the back hallway where the shadows grew longer. He navigated the narrow hallway, the muffled roar of the club's soundcheck fading into a dull, rhythmic throb that he could feel in his teeth. The walls here were lined with framed photos of past performers, their smiling faces obscured by the dim, flickering light of a dying overhead bulb. He reached the door marked *Private* and gave a sharp, rhythmic knock before pushing it open.

Lenny's office was a sharp contrast to the chaotic neon energy outside. It was a windowless box that smelled of expensive leather and stale espresso. Lenny sat behind a glass-topped desk, the glow from three different monitors reflecting off his silk vest and the sharp angles of his face. He looked up, his eyes cold and clinical, as if he were calculating Julius's value in real-time.

"You're on time," Lenny noted, his voice smooth and devoid of any warmth. He didn't rise; he simply gestured to the desk with a gold-tipped pen. "Buddy said you were reliable. He doesn't usually vouch for the 'ROTC' types."

Julius ignored the jab, though he felt a familiar heat rise in his chest. He slid the gym bag onto the glass desk, the heavy *thud* sounding final, like a gavel hitting a block. "Chene Street. Delivered," Julius said, his voice steady.

Lenny pulled the bag toward him. He unzipped it just an inch, his eyes darting across the contents with a practiced, predatory speed. Satisfied, he zipped it back up with a sharp, decisive *zip* that echoed in the small room. He reached into a desk drawer, pulled out a thick envelope, and tossed it onto the glass. It slid across the surface, stopping inches from Julius's hand.

"Your cut," Lenny said, finally leaning back. "You want a drink before you head back to your... other life? We're opening the good stuff for the 'Midnight Royalty' crowd tonight."

Julius looked at the envelope—the literal price of his mother's peace. He felt the weight of the worksheet in his back pocket, the paper crinkling against his hip. *Pause. Breathe.* The "Space Mountain" jokes and the card game at T-Boogie's felt like a lifetime ago. He thought about the sterile, quiet hallway of the tech center where he was headed, and the "plantation" shift that awaited him.

"NAAAA" Julius said, his fingers lingering on the envelope for a second before he tucked it away. "I've got somewhere to be."

"Suit yourself," Lenny muttered, already turning back to his monitors. "Shut the door behind you."

The transition was jarring as Julius stepped out of the office and back through the side entrance. The blinding afternoon sun hit him like a physical weight, and the sudden silence of the alleyway made his ears ring. He climbed into his car, the engine turning over with a tired groan. He was one step closer to the crypt plaque, one step closer to the end of the line, and one step further from the man his mother had raised him to be.

But as his taillights faded into the shimmer of the heat rising off the asphalt, the atmosphere inside the club shifted from mundane preparation to a cold, predatory stillness.

Two men stepped through the front entrance, their presence cutting through the dim, neon-streaked interior like a blade. They wore waist-high, dark blue jackets that seemed to swallow the flickering light of the beer signs. One man, a hulking figure with a face like scarred granite, peeled off from his partner and leaned against the heavy oak door. He crossed his arms, his coat bulging unnaturally over his chest, his eyes scanning the room with the detached boredom of a butcher.

The staff was preoccupied—a bartender was clinking bottles into the well, and a stagehand was untangling a knot of XLR cables near the DJ booth. Nobody witnessed their presence. To the employees, they were just shadows in a room built for shadows.

The second man moved with a terrifying, rhythmic purpose toward the back. He didn't look left or right; he walked straight for Larry's office, his boots thudding softly on the sticky carpet. When he reached the heavy wooden door, he didn't knock. He didn't hesitate.

From beneath the dark folds of his jacket, he produced a silver 47 magnum, the metal dull and oily.

"Hey! You can't be back—" the bartender started to yell, but the words died in his throat.

The man ignored him, leveling the barrel at the door's handle.

BOOM.

The roar of the blast was deafening in the enclosed hallway, a thunderclap that sent a cloud of splintered wood and acorn-sized lead pellets screaming through the air. The lock disintegrated into a spray of jagged metal. The force of the blast kicked the door, causing it to swing partially open on its hinges, groaning as it hit the interior wall.

A heavy, acrid cloud of cordite and burnt wood hung in the air. The man stood in the doorway, the shotgun still smoking, his silhouette framed against the sudden chaos of the club.

Inside the office, the world had just turned into a blizzard of splinters and cordite. Larry had been leaning over a ledger, the tip of his pen hovering over a row of figures, when the door exploded inward. The thunder of the sawed-off shotgun was physical, a wall of sound that slapped the air right out of his lungs.

Larry scrambled back, his chair screeching against the hardwood floor until it hit the heavy mahogany desk. His heart hammered against his ribs like a trapped bird. Through the swirling gray smoke of the doorway, the man in the jacket stepped in, the barrel of the gun still venting a lazy wisp of acrid white vapor.

"The bag, Larry," the man said. It wasn't a question; it was a cold, mechanical command. "Give it up."

Larry's eyes darted to the floor where the heavy duffel sat, then back to the dark bore of the weapon pointed squarely at his sternum. A bitter, hot wave of betrayal washed over him. He'd just seen Julius leave. The timing was too perfect.

"That son of a bitch," Larry hissed, his voice trembling with a mix of terror and pure, unadulterated rage. "Julius set me up! That backstabbing piece of—"

"The bag," the man repeated, his finger tightening on the trigger.

"Fine! Take the damn thing!" Larry spat. He reached down, grunting as he hoisted the weight of the duffel from the floor and slammed it onto the desk. The sound of the cash settling was muffled and heavy. He shoved the bag toward the edge of the desk; his face contorted in a sneer. "Hope you and that coward enjoy it while it lasts. You tell him I'm coming for him!"

The man didn't blink. He didn't care about the politics or the perceived betrayal. He looked at Larry with eyes that were as vacant as a winter sky.

"You won't be coming for anyone," the man said sharply.

BOOM. BOOM. BOOM.

The office, already cramped and hazy, became a kill box. Three successive blasts from the magnum tore into Larry's chest at point-blank range, the sheer kinetic force hurling his body backward. He hit the wood-paneled wall with a sickening thud before sliding down, leaving a dark, jagged smear behind him. His breath left him in a final, wet rattle.

Out in the main room, the world had gone sideways. Leon, who was arrived early for work to setup, didn't wait to see what happened next. His face was pale, his eyes wide with a primal need to survive. He vaulted over the bar, his boots skidding on the polished floor as he lunged for the emergency exit.

He never made it halfway.

The man stationed at the door didn't even uncross his arms to aim. He drew a suppressed handgun from his coat with a fluid, practiced motion.

Thwip.

A single, muffled report echoed through the club. Leon’s head snapped back as the round found its mark. He collapsed instantly, his body skidding a few feet before coming to a dead stop in the center of the dance floor, the neon lights overhead flickering off the growing pool of crimson.

The man at the door holstered his weapon and checked his watch. Silence reclaimed the club, broken only by the hum of the refrigerators and the distant, fading sounds of engines.

The man in the office didn't linger over Larry’s cooling body. He reached out with a gloved hand, snagged the strap of the duffel bag, and hoisted it over his shoulder. The weight of the cash shifted with a dull, muffled thud—the sound of a life traded for a stack of paper.

He stepped over the splintered remains of the doorframe. As he emerged into the main club area, his partner remained a statue by the entrance, his gaze fixed on the back of the dead bartender.

"Clear?" the partner asked, his voice a low, vibrating baritone that barely stirred the air.

"Clear," the gunman replied. He didn't look back at the office. "The mark left just before we hit. Timing was perfect."

The partner nodded once, a sharp, bird-like movement. He reached behind him, pushing the heavy oak door open just a crack to scan the street. The afternoon sun bled into the dark club, illuminating the swirling dust motes and the crimson pool spreading across the dance floor. Outside, the city hummed with indifferent life—traffic moving, people walking, oblivious to the double execution that had just occurred behind the soundproofed walls.

"Car's idling," the partner muttered.

They stepped out into the blinding light. To any passerby, they looked like two businessmen or eccentric locals, their hands tucked deep into their pockets, hiding the heat they carried. They moved with a synchronized, predatory grace toward a nondescript black sedan parked at the curb, its engine purring in a low, steady rhythm.

The gunman tossed the bag into the backseat, the leather upholstery groaning under the weight. He slid into the passenger side while his partner took the wheel.

"Where to?" the driver asked, shifting the car into gear.

The gunman looked at his reflection in the side mirror, adjusting the collar of his coat. A cold, thin smile touched his lips. "Drop the bag at the warehouse then pay a short visit to High-Roller. He's the only loose thread left, and I don't like loose threads."

The sedan pulled away from the curb smoothly, merging into the flow of traffic without a single screech of tires. Behind them, the club sat silent and dark, a tomb waiting to be discovered.

They were barely two blocks away when the first faint wail pierced the afternoon air. It started as a low, mournful pulse in the distance, but quickly sharpened into the frantic, high-pitched scream of multiple units. The driver didn't flinch; his grip on the steering wheel remained relaxed, his eyes tracking the rearview mirror with predatory calm.

As they turned onto the main boulevard, a fleet of blue and red lights crested the hill behind them, reflecting off the sedan's tinted glass. The sirens grew deafening, a chaotic chorus of electronic shrieks that seemed to vibrate the very metal of the car. Two patrol cruisers roared past them in the opposite lane, tires clipping the median as they raced toward the carnage the men had just left behind.

The gunman in the passenger seat watched the blur of chrome and sirens fade in the mirror. He reached down and adjusted the strap of the heavy duffel bag resting against his leg, the sound of the cash shifting beneath the canvas a quiet counterpoint to the fading sirens.

"Response time is getting better," the driver remarked, his voice devoid of emotion as he flicked his turn signal. "Not that it matters now."

The sirens eventually bled into a dull, rhythmic throb, swallowed by the city's indifferent sprawl. The two men disappeared into the midday traffic, two ghosts carrying a bag full of blood money, leaving the law to piece together the wreckage of Leon and Larry lives.

2

By the time Julius stepped onto the platform at OmniTech Corp., his body felt leaden, an anchor dragging him down. A dull, insistent headache throbbed behind his eyes, a counterpoint to the relentless fluorescent murmur of the warehouse. He masked his profound weariness with a practiced, curt nod to the few early coworkers shuffling past.

"Hey Jay," called Vanessa Reviera, Julius's supervisor in the shipping department, her voice bright as she emerged from the breakroom. She held a small, white cup, and a wisp of steam rose from its lip like a smoke signal.

"Tea. Strong," Julius managed a half-smile that didn't quite reach his eyes, accepting the warmth of the ceramic. He took a long, fortifying sip. "Ummm, Do I taste a little Hennesy?" Julius replied in a joking matter.

"Maybe from last night," Vanessa added, her gaze lingering on his tired face. "You, okay?"

"I didn't sleep well the last couple of days, thoughts kept running through my mind," he replied, his voice hoarse, punctuated by an uncontrollable yawn. The sound seemed to echo his internal struggle.

He juggled the mug and his heavy ring of work keys, walking the short distance to his metal workstation. He placed the items on the scarred surface, the keys clinking with a hollow sound. Julius followed Vanessa, her work polo stretched tight across her 5'3 body frame, emphasizing her curves that usually went unnoticed in the radiant glare.

Familiar inventory emails—purchase orders, shipment confirmations—scrolled across his screen, but Julius's mind drifted, pulled by the undertow of fatigue and mixed emotions. It was the same exhaustive feeling that had, in recent nights, driven his late-night compulsions.

"Hey, Jay," Vanessa called, stepping closer to his desk, the cheerful energy she usually carried slightly dimmed by a thread of underlying stress. She placed her hands lightly on the edge of his workstation, her expression shifting from friendly concern to focused seriousness.

"Listen, I know you're running on fumes, and I appreciate you powering through, but I need to talk about those return pallet."

She paused, letting the weight of the task hang in the air. Her eyes, usually so bright, held a sharp, professional intensity now. "It's huge, man. I'm talking about that entire skid of Series 8 devices that got pulled back last week. Remember, those need to be factory reset, thoroughly packaged, and booked out today."

She leaned in just slightly, lowering her voice in a conspiratorial, urgent tone. "If we miss the cut-off time, they're going to treat it as a late return and hit us with a massive restocking/inactivity fee from the manufacturer. You know how unforgiving their accounting is—it's thousands we absolutely cannot afford to eat up right now. Can you try to get a solid head start on the resets before lunch? It's crunch time on this one, Jay. We're on the clock."

Halfway done with the massive pallet, Julius shocked himself out of the fog of near-slumber, and he remembered Dr. Alvarez's plan. He pulled out his phone and tapped out a quick reflection in his note app: "Morning fog. Headache. The urge to escape is high."

He closed his eyes, inhaled deeply, counting slowly to four, holding for four, exhaling for six. The world went silent, the rhythm of his breathing technique momentarily eclipsing the whir of the machines and the distant chatter. A seed of calmness took root, not a victory, but a brief, blessed pause in the storm. For now, it was enough.

He glanced at the digital clock mounted above the racks. The afternoon stretch was almost over, and Julius was able to handle a large part of the pallets. Julius reopened his inbox with renewed purpose, determined to channel his remaining energy into the concrete, crushing numbers of his work tasks rather than the destructive emptiness he had grown to embrace chasing.

Chris Bell, a man who seemed to have grown an inch for every year he'd aged, leaned over his shoulder, his presence sudden and invasive. Julius flinched, smelling the faint but sharp scent of stale coffee and mint on the man's breath. Chris's long, sinewy arm, supported by an equally tall, slightly slumped frame, created a momentary shadow over the monitor, the movement startlingly fast for someone so lanky. "What the fuck, mane!" Julius yelled, jerking in his chair, startled.

"Damn man, you look like you were brought back from hell!" Chris stated that his joke missed the mark completely.

"Mane, I couldn't sleep last night!"

Chris chuckled, a low, coarse sound. "Oh, Maya was putting that W.A.P. on you, huh?"

"Mane, we hadn't fucked in months!" The words were out before Julius could stop them. His exhaustion instantly switched to a flash of frustration—a sudden, hot spike of temper. His hand balled around the cheap plastic of his pencil, and with a small snap, he broke it in two.

"I know we had our problems lately with different work schedules and shit, but damn, can you at least ride a nigga's face once in a while?" he muttered, the frustration bleeding into a desperate plea.

An unexpected coworker, a thin woman from accounting, walked slowly past Julius's station, her eyes and ears raised slightly as she caught the tail end of his last sentence.

"DAMN, do you mind? We're having a conversation over here!" Chris yelled, causing the woman to speed up her pace until she turned the corner.

"Damn, how long had y'all been together?" Chris asked, oblivious to the snapped tension.

"About three years in a couple of months!"

"You think she's cheating on you?"

Julius paused, the idea—unbidden, insidious—flashing through his mind. He shook it off. "Na, she didn't have it in her. We're just going through a rough patch; we'll get it together soon, I hope."

Chris looked around quickly, moving closer and lowering his voice, though it was still a booming whisper. "Take a half day tonight, get a bottle of Don, go home, and wear her ass out. Show her how backed up you are!" he advised, his eyes gleaming with excited purpose.

Julius shook his head, pushing back from his desk. "I couldn't if I wanted to. I used up all my time healing from my mom's death. One more tardiness or absence, I'll get thrown out this bitch!"

"Technically, you won't be tardy or absent! You already worked just about half of your time." Chris followed him as Julius got up to file some documents in the cabinet. "Besides, Craig and I hadn't seen eye to eye since his daughter was crushing on me. Once he heard about that, she got transferred to the headquarters at Northville and put me in his forever shithouse."

Julius felt the cold press of anxiety. Chris's unsolicited advice was always delivered with a dangerous disregard for the rules.

"That's what I'm saying, bro. You have your pick of any lady! But you're too damn nice for your own good!" Chris laughed, his voice ringing with a naivety that made Julius's skin crawl. Chris saw a "nice guy," oblivious to the fact that Julius had carefully constructed his life on a foundation of shadows and secrets. The same jagged chaos that the woman who force herself on him was the very thing fueling Julius's own hypersexual impulses—a hunger for control that no worksheet could ever quite tame.

"Hey Craig, CRAIG!" Chris yelled, waving his hand vigorously in the direction of their manger.

"Why are you asking that muthafucka over here?" Julius quickly responded, his voice low and panicked.

"Just follow my lead!" Chris hissed back.

The click-clack of brown, hard-soled shoes announced Craig's approach, the sound smacking against the concrete floor. Julius could feel Craig's simmering dislike grow bigger the closer he got. Craig Halligan, a compact, wiry man whose posture was aggressively vertical, stopped directly in front of them, his eyes narrowed on Chris.

"Chris, what are you doing here? This isn't your work area?" Craig asked, his voice sharp and laced with an unspoken accusation.

Chris, who was leaning invasively over Julius's shoulder, straightened slowly, his lanky, powerful frame unfolding to tower over the mid-level manager. He offered a wide, unsettling grin. "Just helping Julius out, sir. Thought I'd lend a highly qualified hand."

Julius took a shaky breath, stepping forward. He looked down at his hands, then up at Craig's stony face. "Craig… Actually, I was hoping to talk to you. I'm not feeling good. Like, at all. I was wondering if I could leave early this evening?"

Craig's face tightened. He glanced dismissively at the monitor showing the serial numbers, then back to Chris. "I'll look over the numbers and get back to you, Julius. In the meantime, Chris, get back to your station!"

Chris slowly raised one foot, held it suspended for a beat, and then slammed the hard sole down onto the concrete. The sound was a loud, deliberate punctuation mark. He then raised his right arm in a dramatic, sweeping arc, his fingers touching his forehead in a ridiculous, exaggerated salute.

"Aye, aye, Captain!" Chris drawled, the sarcasm heavy enough to hang in the air like exhaust.

Without waiting for a response, he spun around, turning his back to Craig. He paused only long enough to raise one leg high behind him before letting it tap back to the floor, then swaggered off toward his workstation, clearly relishing the silent fury he'd sparked in his manager.

Craig watched him go; his jaw was clenched so tight that Julius thought he might crack a tooth. About twenty minutes later, Julius was meticulously sorting cables when his phone buzzed. It was an internal call—Craig Halligan displayed on the screen.

Julius took a deep breath before answering. "Yeah, Craig?"

"Listen, I talked to Vanessa," Craig said, his tone clipped and purely transactional. "She's up to speed on… everything. She needed to approve it, but when it's good with her, then you can leave."

Julius felt a surge of relief mixed with irritation at the curtness. "Thanks, Craig, I appreciate you following up on—"

Click.

The line went dead. Craig had hung up before Julius could finish the sentence.

Julius stared at the phone screen, shaking his head. "Fuckboy," he muttered, the insult half-joking, half-genuine. The man had the grace of a broken vending machine.

Moments later, after quickly visiting the restroom, Julius came out and spotted Vanessa leaving a colleague's desk from afar. "Vanessa, can I grab you for just a second?" he asked, trying to sound earnest and apologetic.

She turned, her expression already soft with concern. She was genuinely kind. Julius began, lowering his voice. "I'm still feeling pretty wiped. I know you and Craig talked about me heading out, but I wanted to make sure you were officially okay with me taking off?"

Vanessa's face immediately shifted to one of deep sympathy. "Oh, Julius, of course, you needed to go. Don't worry about the inventory, we can handle it. I saw you did a big bulk of the laptops yourself."

Julius managed a pained, grateful expression. "Thank you, Vanessa. I really appreciate you're understanding."

"Go. Please, go," she urged, giving his arm a brief, comforting squeeze. "Take care of yourself."

"Will do. Thank you again."

Julius quickly retreated to his pod, grabbed his work bag, and didn't look back. He began walking toward the main exit, already feeling the weight of the building lift off his shoulders as he approached the doors.

As Julius pushed through the glass doors of the building and stepped out into the crisp evening air, the weight of the lie—and the job itself—began to dissipate. He had enough energy to finish his shift. Yet, a little knot of guilt still pulled at his stomach.

He quickly rationalized it: it was a harmless little heist of time, and he was tired of working under Craig's scrutiny. The feeling morphed from guilt into a daring sense of freedom—a sensation not unlike sneaking out of class in high school. He had successfully ditched work, and the thrill of the deception was now mixing deliciously with excitement.

His mind raced ahead, skipping the commute and landing squarely on the thought of his girlfriend. He pictured her face, the way she smiled, and the instant, easy comfort of her presence. The thought of spending the unexpected extra hours with her, unburdened by work deadlines or Craig's simmering disdain, was intoxicating.

Julius drove through the city, the earlier little knot of guilt completely forgotten, replaced by pure, humming anticipation. The evening drive with the window down made him feel a lot better. The cool air rushing in felt like a genuine escape. He glanced at the blurred streaks of light outside—the city blurred past, lights smeared by rain. His fuel gauge was dangerously low; his tank was almost empty.

The last trace of work anxiety vanished as he decided on his first stop: Meijer's. He needed to set the mood. Pulling into the parking lot after getting gas, he felt a definite shift in focus. This wasn't about work anymore; it was about pleasure. He walked into the store and headed straight for the wine aisle, carefully selecting a deep, velvety red wine—something smooth and rich.

As he stood in the checkout line, the bottle cool in his hand and an individual red rose ready, the excitement became palpable. He was then just minutes away from his apartment, Maya, and the promise of a long, intimate evening. Julius parked and checked the dash clock. The time of 9:20 pm was displayed on the radio before he exited his car. He grabbed the wine, rose, and his work bag, the excitement still thrumming beneath the surface.

The heel of Julius's shoe clicked a rhythmic, confident beat against the hallway tile. He was home. Juggling the bottle of wine in one arm, he fumbled with his keys until the metal teeth finally caught. He slid the deadbolt back with a satisfying *thunk*. The door swung open, but the air in the apartment felt wrong. A muffled gasp cut through the quiet—a sharp, staccato sound that wasn't his, and certainly wasn't the warm welcome he'd envisioned.

Julius froze while putting his work bag on the floor. His breathing slowed, the instinct to turn and flee warring with a cold, dreadful curiosity. He forced himself into a mask of calm, inhaling the familiar, mocking scent of blueberry lavender as he moved toward the stairs. As he reached the upper corridor, the sound reached him: faint moans and the rhythmic rustle of sheets drifting from behind his bedroom door. The thrum of excitement that had carried him home from work curdled instantly into a thunderous, panicked pulse.

His steps became hushed, involuntary, as if he were navigating the landscape of a fever dream. He leaned his weight against the frame and nudged the door just enough to see. Through the gauzy, filtered light, his world shattered. There was Maya, her dark hair fanning across the satin pillows, the arch of her back rising and falling in rhythm with another man. The sight hit Julius with the physical force of a lead pipe to the gut. His blood turned to ice.

A voice inside him screamed for silence, for retreat, for a different reality, but his body moved on a track of raw, ancient rage. He kicked the door wide. It hit the stopper with a violent bang.

"Julius—no, please—!" Maya shrieked, scrambling backward.

The man lurched upright, his eyes wide and vacant with panic. Adrenaline snapped in Julius's veins like a live wire. Maya struggled to grab the bed sheet, trying to hide the sin of her naked body. He dropped the rose, but it didn't matter.

His fist was already moving. With all his might, he connected with a sickening, wet *thud* against the man's jaw, sending him reeling.

"Is this what you were doing?" Julius's voice was a jagged edge.

"While I was out building a future for us?"

Maya scrambled to the edge of the bed, clutching the sheets to her chest as her left breast slid past her arm. Her voice shook, vibrating between frantic sobs and useless pleas.

"Julius, I—it's not what you think!"

But Julius's vision had tunneled. He stared down at the crumpled figure at his feet. His knuckles burned, a thin trail of crimson trickling from a split in his skin.

"Every lunch break call that went unanswered," he whispered, his voice trembling with the weight of a dozen realizations.

"That telltale cologne. You blamed the neighbor."

Maya rose to her knees on the mattress, her eyes wild with desperation.

"I was lost. I'm sorry—"

Julius's chest heaved. He didn't wait for the rest. He turned, crossing the room in three long, predatory strides. He yanked the closet door open and grabbed the duffel bag he usually reserved for weekend trips.

"Julius, please don't go," Maya sobbed, her voice breaking.

"We can fix this—"

"What's there to fix?" He stormed back toward the bed, grabbing clothes in handfuls and shoving them into the bag in haphazard folds.

"I still love you!" she cried.

Julius stopped mid-motion, his hand poised over the open zipper. When he spoke, his voice cracked like glass under a heavy boot.

"Love doesn't look like lies, Maya. It doesn't sound like moans through a locked door."

Maya sank to the floor beside the unconscious man, burying her face in her hands. Julius pulled the zipper shut. Each click of the metal teeth sounded like a nail being driven into a coffin. He hoisted the bag over his shoulder, his boots echoing like thunder on the hardwood.

"I hope he was worth it," he said, his tone turning deathly cold as he picked up his work bag.

Maya's sobs filled the space, a hollow, haunting sound that followed him to the threshold, grabbing his work bag. He paused, hand on the knob, and looked back one last time—at the shredded sheets, the disarray, and her broken shape on the floor. The image seared itself into his mind, a brand he knew would never fade.

"Goodbye, Maya," he said, the name sounding foreign on his lips.

He closed the door gently behind him, leaving the scent of betrayal and lavender to waft through the silence of a ruined home. The hallway swallowed him whole. His escape from work had been successful, but his escape from this life had only just begun. The ache inside him remained—a sharp, blinding pain where, only moments ago, there had been hope.

The guilt was then a faint, distant whisper, drowned out by the anticipation of getting close and reveling in the unexpected, stolen hours of love and relaxation. Julius stood frozen in the hallway, the backpack suddenly feeling less like luggage and more like a dead weight chained to his arm. The shock started to recede, leaving behind a terrifying vacuum filled only by heartbreak, searing anger, and absolute solitude.

For close to three years, he had poured his heart and soul into that apartment, into Maya, and into a future he was actively building—even risking his job that day, in part, for the promise of a quiet, intimate evening with her. He had done everything he thought was right: working the hours, planning the life, loving her fiercely. Now, the moans, the scent of lavender and strange cologne, and her desperate, meaningless pleas were an agonizing soundtrack to the wreckage of his devotion.

He blinked, the harsh hallway light revealing the glistening on his cheeks. They were tears, but they were quickly drying under the heat of his rising fury. Three years. He had wasted three years on a lie that was just exposed in the most brutal, humiliating way possible.

His first action was primal: he needed distance and air. He didn't bother with the elevator. He found the nearest stairwell door, pushed it open with his shoulder, and began to descend the concrete stairs two at a time, the *thud-thud-thud* of his boots an angry, uneven rhythm echoing his frantic pulse. He couldn't stay in the confines of the building that held her and the scent of betrayal. He needed the anonymity of the street, the cold indifference of the city. He needed to be anywhere but here.

The hollow thud in his chest had nothing to do with the car. It had been there for thirty minutes, ever since he'd walked in on three years of his life dissolving in his own bedroom.

"I just don't get it, Jaz," Julius said, his voice raw. The steering wheel of his Honda felt slick under his pale-knuckled grip. Rain began to speckle the windshield, blurring the endless river of red taillights on the 94-West freeway.

"What's not to get, Julius?" His sister's voice crackled through the car's Bluetooth, sharp with a familiar, protective anger.

"She's a sociopath bitch. I never liked her. You're driving? Julius, pull over. You sound awful."

"I'm fine. I just... I had to get out of there. The smell of them, Jaz. It was..." He squeezed his eyes shut for a second, just one second, to banish the image of Maya and... he didn't even know the guy's name.

"Julius, listen to me. You are in shock. You should not be driving on the freeway in this weather and your condition—"

A black shape torpedoed into his peripheral vision. There was no time to react. A high-end BMW, flying in the fast lane, suddenly hydroplaned on the fresh slick of rain. It fishtailed wildly, its headlights cutting a chaotic arc across the lanes. Julius slammed his brakes, but he was already part of the equation he couldn't solve.

The world became a symphony of violence. First, there was the sickening CRUNCH as the BMW's rear quarter-panel clipped his front fender. Julius's car shot sideways, tires screaming, into the concrete median. The *WHOMP* of his airbag deploying was like a punch to the face, stealing his breath and filling the car with a chalky, acrid smoke. His chest exploded in pain as the seatbelt locked, crushing his ribs.

He was pinned against the barrier, dazed, ears ringing. The last thing he saw before the world stopped making sense was the BMW. It didn't just spin; it hit the median at a terrible angle, launched into the air, and barrel-rolled. It was a physics-defying horror show of shattering glass and crumpling metal, finally coming to rest twenty yards ahead of him, completely upside down, on its roof.

The silence that followed was worse. It was a heavy, wet blanket, broken only by the *tink... tink... tink* of his own cooling engine and the distant sound of horns from the traffic grinding to a halt behind them.

"What the FUCK...Jaz?" he wheezed. No answer. The call was dead.

He fumbled for the seatbelt release, his fingers numb. It clicked open, and he slumped forward, gasping. The pain in his chest was a bonfire. He shoved the deflated airbag aside and kicked at his door. It groaned and bent, but opened six inches. He squeezed his way out, stumbling onto the dark, wet pavement.

The freeway was a parking lot. People were emerging from their cars, silhouetted against their headlights with phones out. Julius ignored them. He ignored the fire in his ribs. He limped, then staggered, toward the black, inverted ruin of the BMW. Steam hissed from its undercarriage.

"Hey!" he yelled, his voice cracking. "Hey, man! Are you...?"

He reached the driver's side window, or what was left of it. The man inside was hanging upside down, held by his seatbelt. He was wearing a dark, expensive-looking suit, now ruined. His head was slumped forward at an unnatural angle. From a massive, jagged gash on his forehead, a thick, dark stream of blood ran up his face, pooling in his hairline. His eyes were closed.

"Sir!" Julius yelled, panic rising thick in his throat, tasting like airbag dust. "Hey! Wake up! Can you hear me?"

He reached a shaky hand through the shattered window, stopping inches from the man's face. He was afraid to touch him, afraid of what he might find. "Wake up, dammit!"

The man didn't move. He was completely, terrifyingly still. The betrayal, Maya, the argument—it all evaporated. There was only this: the inverted car, the smell of gasoline, and the unconscious man. Julius scrambled for the phone in his pocket. The screen was a spiderweb of cracks, but it lit up. He jabbed 9-1-1.

"911, what is your emergency?"

"Accident. A bad one," Julius panted, clutching his chest. "On 94-West, just past the Beaubien exit. A car flipped. It's... it's on its roof. The driver's unconscious. He's bleeding. Badly."

"Sir, are you involved in the accident?"

"Yes! My car hit the barrier. I'm... I think I'm okay. But the other guy. Please, you have to hurry. He's not moving."

"Help is on the way, sir. We have units on route now. Is he breathing?"

Julius leaned closer, squinting into the dark cabin.

"I... I can't tell. There's so much blood. Just... just send someone. Fast."

He stayed on the line, answering her questions numbly, his eyes fixed on the man in the suit. The wait felt like an eternity, each second stretching out, filled with the growing wail of distant sirens.

In what felt like both a lifetime and no time at all, the night exploded in red and blue. The *whoop-whoop* of sirens became a deafening wall of sound. Two police cruisers, a fire truck, and two ambulances arrived, flooding the scene with light.

"Clear the area! Move back!" a police officer shouted, already laying out flares. Paramedics swarmed the BMW with heavy tools.

"We need the Jaws! Full C-spine precaution!"

Another paramedic, a woman with a kind but serious face, rushed to Julius.

"Sir, you were in this? Are you hurt?"

"My chest," Julius gasped, the adrenaline beginning to fade, letting the pain rush in. "My chest... the seatbelt. But him... is he...?"

"They're working on him. Let me look at you." She shined a bright light in his eyes, making him wince.

"You've got a nasty contusion from that airbag. I want you to sit down. Right now."

As she took his blood pressure, a police officer approached, his notepad illuminated by the flashing lights.

"Sir, I'm Officer Mendez. Can you tell me what happened?"

Julius tried to focus. The world was tilting. "I... I was in the middle lane. He came from the left. Fast. It's raining... he just... he lost it. He hit me. I hit the wall. He... he flipped."

"Were you on your phone, sir?"

The question landed like a stone. "I... yes. But it was Bluetooth. Hands-free. I was talking to my sister."

"Were you distracted?"

Julius looked from the officer to the wreck, where the team was now cutting the roof off the BMW. He thought of Maya's face, the sick lurch in his stomach.

"My girlfriend… she…" He stopped. He shook his head, the motion making him dizzy. "Yes. I was distracted. I was upset. But I was in my lane. He hit me."

"We'll get statements from the witnesses," the officer said, his voice neutral.

"They've got him!" a firefighter yelled.

Julius watched as they carefully extracted the man in the suit, now on a backboard, his head immobilized in a bright orange brace. A paramedic was bagging him, forcing air into his lungs. As they wheeled the gurney past, Julius saw his face, pale and slack under the blood. He was still unconscious.

"Officer," the paramedic attending to Julius said sharply, "we're taking him."

"What?" Julius asked, confused.

"You're coming with us," she said, strapping an oxygen mask to his face. "

Your heart rate is all over the place, you have a probable concussion, and I don't like the sound of your breathing. You could have a punctured lung or broken ribs."

They loaded him onto a separate gurney, into the second ambulance.

"What about him?" Julius asked, his voice muffled by the mask, as they began to wheel him away.

"You both are going to Henry Ford," the paramedic said.

As they closed the ambulance doors, the last thing Julius saw was his own mangled Honda, its nose crushed against the barrier. The pain from his chest and the pain from his life had blurred into one single, throbbing, overwhelming ache. He was alone in the back of an ambulance, speeding away from a disaster he wasn't sure he hadn't caused.

The sudden slam of the ambulance doors marked a complete separation from the wreckage, the police lights, and the shattered pieces of his life. Lying strapped to the gurney, his world was reduced to the violent rocking of the vehicle, the antiseptic smell of the interior, and the insistent whine of the siren—a sound that seemed to be directly inside his skull.

The paramedic, the kind but serious woman who had treated him on the freeway, was named Sarah. She worked quickly and efficiently, her movements in the cramped space both professional and jarringly close.

The oxygen mask clamped over his face felt suffocating, yet the air it delivered was his only lifeline. The pain in his chest, where the seatbelt had crushed him against the impact, intensified with every movement. The world was a blur of sterile white light and the rhythmic, artificial hiss of a ventilator. Julius's voice came out as a strained rasp, muffled by the plastic oxygen mask fogging against his face.

"My ribs..." he wheezed, each word a battle against the constriction in his chest. "They feel... broken."

Sarah leaned into his field of vision. Her face was a mask of professional composure, her voice a calm anchor in the sea of his rising panic.

"We're checking for that right now, Julius," she said, her hands moving with practiced efficiency over the bedside controls. "We've already administered pain medication through your IV, but it's going to take a minute to fully kick in. Right now, I need you to focus. Your only priority is to try and breathe normally."

She reached down, adjusting the blood pressure cuff strapped to his arm as the machine began to cycle with a mechanical whir.

"Your heart rate is still dangerously high, and we need to rule out a pneumothorax—a collapsed lung," she explained, her eyes darting briefly to the glowing vitals on the monitor.

She gave him a small, reassuring nod, though her focus remained clinical.

"Your systolic pressure is holding for now, but we're keeping a very close eye on your respiratory rate. Just stay with me. Keep breathing."

The sirens were a continuous, overwhelming shriek. Julius couldn't distinguish the noise from the tinnitus in his ears caused by the airbag deployment. He felt a wave of nausea, a dizzying side effect of the probable concussion. He closed his eyes, but the internal chaos was worse than the external.

The physical disaster hadn't cured the heartbreak; it had merely paused it. Now, in the dark, rocking isolation of the ambulance, the memories came flooding back, overlaying the present pain.

He saw Maya's face—not the guilty face in the bedroom, but her earlier, loving face—followed immediately by the jarring image of her arched back and the stranger's panic. The memory of the blueberry lavender scent battled with the smell of burnt oil and airbag dust still clinging to his clothes. He recalled telling Officer Mendez he was “distracted”—a distraction caused by fidelity being wiped out in one brutal moment. The sense of profound, all-consuming shame and grief was now competing directly with the intense pain in his chest. Julius realized the irony: he had successfully lied and planned a glorious, intimate escape only to have his entire life, personal and romantic, detonate simultaneously.

“Did they...” Julius’s voice was a ghost of a sound, choked by the dryness in his throat and the plastic of the mask. His eyes searched Sarah's, clouded with a sudden, jarring clarity.

“Did they get the other driver out?”

Sarah’s hands didn't pause as she checked the line on his IV, but her gaze softened just enough to acknowledge the question.

“Yes, Julius,” she said firmly. “They extracted him. He’s currently en route, the same as you.”

She stepped closer, placing a steadying hand near his shoulder to ground him. "Our focus is you right now. You've been through a massive trauma. Try not to talk—just focus on the air coming in and out."

He lay back, utterly defeated. He was alone. The person he would normally call in a crisis was the reason for the crisis. The stolen afternoon, the red wine now shattered glass and spilled liquid in his car, had led only to this: a gurney, a mask, and the terrifying sound of a siren speeding him toward an uncertain fate. The crushing weight of the seatbelt had cracked his ribs, but the betrayal had shattered his foundation. The ambulance finally decelerated, the siren winding down into a slow, pulsating whoop.

"We're here, Julius. Level One trauma center. Just a few more minutes, and we'll get you settled."

The doors burst open, and the brilliant, cold white light of the Henry Ford Emergency Bay flooded the compartment, a harsh, undeniable signal that his life had changed forever.

The ambulance bay at Henry Ford Hospital was a choreographed storm. The first ambulance, the one carrying the man in the suit, barely stopped before the doors were thrown open. A trauma team was already waiting on the tarmac, their faces grim under the harsh floodlights.

"Male, 40s, GCS 5 on scene, dropped to 3 in transport!" the paramedic shouted, running alongside the gurney as it flew through the trauma bay doors. "Unresponsive, severe TBI, BP is 80 over 40 and dropping. We've got two wide-bore IVs in!"

"Neuro is scrubbed in, take him straight up to OR 3!" a surgeon commanded, his voice muffled by his mask. "Move, people, move!" The gurney, and the team surrounding it, vanished down the hall in a desperate sprint.

Moments later, the second ambulance pulled in with less frenzy, but no less urgency. Julius was wheeled out, an oxygen mask fogging with his shallow, pained breaths. He was conscious, his eyes wide and tracking the ceiling lights.

"Driver two," the second paramedic reported to a triage nurse. "Stable, but complaining of 10-out-of-10 chest pain, probable rib fractures, possible pneumo. Head contact with the airbag, watch for concussion."

"Take him to Bay 12," the nurse directed calmly. "Let's get him on a monitor, full workup. Dr. Chen will be right with him."

3

The waiting areas hummed with anxiety. In a small, windowless "Family Consultation" room near the surgical wing, three women sat in stiff, beige chairs waiting for news about a patience named Daniel Vance. He was the person involved in the accident, the one whose life now hung in the balance just a few hallways away.

One, an older woman named Ms. Eleanor Vance, was frail, her hands twisting a damp tissue into knots. Beside her sat Eleanor's daughter and Daniel's younger sister, Mary Vance; her eyes were red-rimmed and swollen, her gaze fixed vacantly on the door as she leaned toward her mother in a silent, supportive vigil. The third, Cynthia Townsend, Daniel's boss, was sharp, dressed in a business suit that was only slightly wrinkled from her rush to the hospital. She stared at the sterile tile floor, her jaw tight, looking like a stark, corporate contrast to the raw, familial grief filling the small space.

A hospital liaison—a woman with a kind face and a practiced, sad smile—had just appeared from behind the double doors, leaving a trail of devastating clinical facts in her wake.

"Mr. Vance is in surgery," she had explained, her voice low.

"He has a severe head injury. Dr. Ibrahim is with him now. It's... it's a very serious operation. We will give you an update the second we have one."

Now, silence filled the small waiting room, thick and suffocating. Cynthia stared at the beige wall, her mind reeling. To the world—and to the grieving mother, Eleanor, sitting beside her—Daniel Vance was a dedicated public servant, a rising star in Detroit's Community Relations Department. He was the "hospital liaison" who smoothed over crises and built bridges. But Cynthia knew the truth. She knew the man who didn't work for the city, but for her, playing the part of the polished, high-end escort who occupied female client beds and her secrets.

"He was supposed to close the Kellinger deal tonight," Cynthia said. Her voice was hollow, the lie tasting like ash. She wasn't really speaking to Eleanor, but to the empty air of the room. "He... he just bought that car. A 7-series. He was so proud of it."

It was a car bought with the proceeds of his secret life, a trophy of a career his family didn't even know he had.

Eleanor let out a sound like a small, wounded bird. "My Daniel... he drives too fast. I always told him, 'Daniel, you drive too fast.' He never listens..." She bowed her head, dissolving into quiet, racking sobs that shook her fragile frame.

Cynthia looked profoundly uncomfortable, the weight of her shared history with Daniel pressing against the innocence of the woman next to her. She reached out, placing a stiff, hesitant hand on the mother's shoulder. "They are doing everything they can, Eleanor," Cynthia whispered, though she wondered if "everything" would ever be enough to fix the shattered glass and shattered lives.

Across the hallway of the main Emergency Department waiting room, Jazmine Sterling burst through the automatic doors. Her hair was plastered to her head from the rain, her eyes wild with panic. The call had dropped, replaced by a terrible silence, and then a call from a state trooper using Julius's phone had confirmed her worst fears. She ran to the glass-fronted reception desk, bypassing a man holding a bloody towel to his hand.

"My brother!" she gasped, her voice cracking. "He was in an accident on the 94. Julius Sterling. They brought him here!"

The receptionist, a large woman who looked entirely unfazed, held up a single, placating hand. "Honey, I need you to breathe. I can't help you if you're screaming. What's the name?"

"Sterling!" Jazmine said, tears of frustration welling. "Julius Sterling. S-T-E-R-L-I-N-G. He was... he was driving a Honda."

The receptionist's fingers tapped on the keyboard, the sound agonizingly slow. "Okay, I see him."

Jazmine sagged against the counter, her knees weak with a sudden, tidal wave of relief. "Oh GOD! Is he okay? Where is he?"

"He's still in the ER. He's stable and being seen by a doctor right now," the woman said, her voice softening slightly. "They're checking on some chest pain."

Jazmine's mind was racing, connecting the emotional devastation of his call with the physical violence of the crash. "Can I see him? Please?"

"You can go back," the receptionist nodded, giving her a name tag and buzzing the lock on the doors to her left.

"Go through those double doors, make a left, and look for the signs to Bay 12. A nurse will meet you there. Just one visitor for now."

Jazmine shoved the heavy door open, stepping from the relative quiet of the waiting room into the stark, bright chaos of the ER. The air smelled of antiseptic and something metallic. A symphony of beeps, rushed footsteps, and hushed, urgent conversations filled her ears. She hurried past curtains hiding other people's emergencies, her heart hammering against her own ribs, following the signs for Bay 12, praying for what she would find.

Jazmine found him in Bay 12. She pulled back the thin, pale blue curtain and the world stopped spinning. Julius was sitting up on the edge of the gurney, his shirt open. A web of EKG leads was stuck to his chest, and a clear IV line snaked into the back of his hand, dripping saline. His skin was pale, but the thing that made her stomach clench was the violent, diagonal stripe of purple and red that crossed his torso—a perfect, raw abrasion from the seatbelt.

"Oh god, Julius," she breathed, rushing forward.

He looked up, his eyes hollowed out by shock and pain. "Jaz... Hey. You made it."

"Of course I made it." She touched his arm, her fingers trembling. "They just said 'chest pain.' This..."

"It's just bruised," he grunted, wincing as he shifted. "Feels like I got kicked by a fucking mule, but nothing's broken. Where's... where's Leo? Is he okay?"

"He's with Mrs. Petrov," Jazmine said, her voice tight as she pulled the metal-legged visitor's chair closer. The scrape it made on the linoleum was a high, thin scream. "He was fast asleep before I left. He's fine. You're the one I'm worried about."

Julius nodded, closing his eyes for a second. "Good. Good."

A hard silence settled between them. Jazmine's relief began to curdle into the anger she'd felt on the phone. "That... woman," she spat. "I have wanted to whoop her ass for a long time, Jay. Now, I have a reason..."

A small, painful laugh, more like a cough, escaped him. "What's your short ass gonna to do to her? Upper cut her kneecaps?"

Jazmine's eyes flashed. She gave him a look of death. "You know I hate when you talk about my height. Just for that, I'm going to kick your cripple ass when we get home!"

"My bad, my bad," Julius said, raising a hand in surrender, the gesture pulling at his ribs. "Just... trying to break the tension."

The antiseptic smell of the ER was failing. Over the sharp scent of bleach and rubbing alcohol, a heavy, organic funk began to seep through the thin fabric of the privacy curtains. In the bay directly next to Julius, the rhythmic squeak of a gurney was punctuated by low, guttural groans that sounded less like vocalizations and more like a physical struggle.

"Oh, god," a voice strained from behind the curtain, thick with desperation. "Please... the bedpan. I need it *NOW, oh shit.*"

There were a frantic scuffle of footsteps and the clatter of plastic against metal. "We're coming, Mr. Henderson! Just hold on," a nurse hissed, her voice tight with the stress of a crowded shift. As soon as the nurse came back with a bed pan a wet, explosive sound erupted from the next bay, followed by a long, harrowing groan of relief and agony. Jazmine's nose crinkled, and she pulled the collar of her sweater over her face.

A doctor in blue scrubs stepped into the area, holding a tablet. He looked tired, his eyes darting briefly toward the neighboring curtain as another series of loud, rhythmic splashes and grunts filled the air. He cleared his throat, trying to maintain a professional veneer.

A doctor in blue scrubs stepped into the area, holding a tablet. "Mr. Sterling? I'm Dr. Chen. Got your X-rays back. Good news. No fractures, no breaks. You have some severely bruised ribs and a nasty contusion from the belt, but nothing's punctured. The nurse will give you some medication, a work release, and will discharge you with a prescription for some serious painkillers."

"Mr. Sterling? I'm Dr. Chen." He had to raise his voice to compete with a particularly loud straining sound from Mr. Henderson. "Got your... X-rays back."

Splat.

Dr. Chen winced but kept going. "Good news. No fractures, no breaks. You have some severely bruised ribs and a nasty contusion from the belt, but nothing's punctured."

Julius tried to focus on the doctor's words, but his eyes kept drifting toward the curtain divider, which was vibrating slightly from the activity on the other side. A foul, sulfurous odor was now undeniable, thick enough to taste.

"The nurse will give you some medication," Chen continued, his voice wavering as a chorus of "Oh, heavens" and more liquid sounds drowned him out. "A work release... and will discharge you with... a prescription for some serious painkillers."

"Thank you, Doctor," Julius said, relief washing over his face, though he was breathing through his mouth to survive the atmosphere. "Jazmine, can you get my shirt from the table? Let's get the fuck out of here before they blow an ass cheek."

As she helped him ease his arms into his shirt, trying to shield him from the increasingly graphic auditory experience next door, two uniformed police officers appeared at the curtain.

"Mr. Sterling?" the first one said, though he immediately paused, his nostrils flaring as he took in the scent of the room. He looked at his partner with wide eyes. "I'm Officer Diaz. This is Officer Krupke. We... uh... we need to get your official statement."

From the next bay, a final, thunderous groan of "Thank you, Jesus!" echoed through the ward, followed by the unmistakable sound of a bedpan being whisked away.

Julius winced, slowly buttoning the shirt over his raw skin. "Yeah. Okay. I... I told the officer at the scene. He came out of nowhere. Hydroplaned right in front of me."

"We're just corroborating, sir," Officer Diaz said, his pen poised over a small notepad. "We see no signs of impairment. Your story matches the witness accounts." He looked up. "Just a bad night."

"The other driver," Julius said, his voice suddenly small. "The man in the BMW. Is he... is he okay?"

Diaz and Krupke shared a look, a brief, professional flicker that spoke volumes. "He was taken into surgery upon arrival," Krupke said, his voice carefully neutral. He leaned in a fraction, lowering his tone. "But between us, Mr. Sterling... it doesn't look good."

Down the hall, in the sterile quiet of the surgical waiting room, the door opened. Dr. Ibrahim entered, his mask hanging from his neck, his face etched with exhaustion. Cynthia stood immediately. Beside her, Eleanor gripped the armrests of her chair, and Daniel's sister, Tisha, held her hand.

"Mrs. Vance," the doctor began, his voice heavy. "We did... we did everything we could to save his life."

The mother let out a high, thin gasp. "No..."

"The impact caused massive internal injuries," the doctor continued, his words kind but direct. "We couldn't stop the bleeding. I'm so very sorry. Mr. Vance passed on the operating table."

"NO!" The mother's gasp turned into a primal wail. She collapsed forward, caught by her daughter, who was now sobbing silently, bracing her mother's weight. "Not my Daniel! Not my baby boy!"

Cynthia moved quickly, helping the daughter guide Eleanor back into the chair. She knelt before them, her professional poise a strange anchor in the storm of grief.

"Eleanor, listen to me," Cynthia said, her voice firm but compassionate. "I am here. You are not alone. We will handle everything. The funeral, the repass... everything. Daniel's savings... he had a substantial portfolio. It will all go to you. You don't have to worry about a thing."

She consoled them for another minute, then, with a final squeeze of the daughter's shoulder, she stood and slipped out of the room. The air in the hallway was cold, a welcome shock. She wiped a tear from her face, pulling her phone from her purse, and hit a speed-dial number.

"It's me," she said, her voice low. "He's gone, Dominic. Daniel died on the table... Yes. A tragedy." She paced, listening. "I don't know what happened. I was at the office; I got the call... Yes, of course. He was a good man."

Dominic Preston, Cynthia's partner in the lavish lifestyle, tinny voice crackled on the other end. "A good man, yes. But Cynthia, what about the business? The passive income? We have clients..."

"I don't *know*, Dominic," she hissed. "We'll have to find..."

Her gaze landed down the hall. She saw him. The other driver. He was standing by the ER exit, talking to the two officers. His sister was at his side. He was just finishing buttoning his shirt, and as he moved, the harsh fluorescent light caught the defined, sweating muscles of his abdomen.

"Mr. Sterling, you're free to go," Officer Diaz was saying. "But don't leave town. We'll need to know where you are in case, we have more questions."

Julius nodded numbly. "Don't worry, I'll be at my sister's." A nurse handed him a packet of papers.

Cynthia watched him, her eyes narrowing. He was tall, with a brawny, powerful stature, and a face that was strikingly handsome even when pale and bruised.

"Dominic," she said into the phone, her voice changing, a sudden spark of calculation in it. "I think I might have just found a replacement. I'll call you back."

She disconnected the call just as the officers turned to leave. "Officers Diaz, Krupke," she said, stepping forward.

"Director Townsend," Diaz replied, recognizing her city title. "A bad night to be here."

"Awful." She gestured with her chin toward Julius, who was now walking slowly, protectively, with his sister toward the exit. "Was that the other party involved?"

"Yeah," Krupke said. "No alcohol, no drugs. Just a good guy in a bad situation. Said he just found out his girlfriend was cheating on him, was on the phone with his sister, and... boom."

Cynthia's eyebrow raised. "That's not his girlfriend with him?"

"No, that's the sister. He's staying with her," Diaz added. "Man had a bad night all around."

Cynthia looked back at the consultation room, where the sound of weeping was still audible, then at the officers. "Well," she said, her voice flat. "It just got worse. The man he hit... Mr. Vance... he died. About ten minutes ago."

Both officers winced, letting out a simultaneous sound of dismay. "Och," Diaz muttered, running a hand over his face. "Damn."

Cynthia barely registered their reaction. Her eyes were glued to Julius's back. She watched his tall, handsome frame as he and his sister pushed through the double doors and disappeared into the rainy night. The automatic doors of the ER hissed shut behind them, sealing off the sterile brightness and antiseptic smell. The night air was damp and cold, a shock to his system. Julius moved stiffly, each step a careful negotiation with his screaming ribs.

"My car..." he said, his voice a gravelly monotone as they walked under the dim parking lot lights. "The way I hit that divider... it's gone. Totaled."

"It's just metal, Jay," Jazmine said, hitting the unlock button on her key fob. Her small sedan chirped in response. "You're alive. That's all that matters. Get in."

He grunted as he lowered himself into the passenger seat, the seatbelt a new kind of torture as he clicked it into place. The drive started in silence, just the rhythmic *thwack-thwack* of the wipers clearing the fine mist.

"Okay," Jazmine said finally, her eyes fixed on the empty road. "At the hospital, I didn't push. But you have to talk to me. On the phone, before the crash... you sounded like your world was ending. What all happened, Julius?"

Julius let his head fall back against the headrest, staring at the dark ceiling. "You want the context?" he sighed, and the breath hitched in his chest. "I... I have to start from the beginning."

He told her. He told her everything, the words spilling out in a dull, factual stream, as if he were reading a police report. Coming home early. The sounds from the bedroom. Kicking the door open. Maya, and some guy he'd never seen, tangled in *his* sheets. The yelling. The pathetic, "It's not what it looks like." Grabbing his keys, storming out, just driving. "And then," he finished, his voice cracking, "I called you. And I was... I was so angry, Jaz. I wasn't watching. And then... just headlights. Everywhere."

Jazmine's hands were bone-white on the steering wheel. "That... *bitch*," she hissed, her voice vibrating with a cold fury. "I always knew it. I told you; I *told* you she was no good."

"Yeah, well. You were right." He looked out the window as they pulled into her townhouse complex. "You were right."

Cynthia pulled her phone away from her ear, the distant, tinny voice of her partner, Dominic Preston, now utterly irrelevant. Her eyes remained locked on the swinging double doors where Julius and his sister had just disappeared. Daniel Vance, her client and business partner, was dead, and the immense pressure of their failing portfolio and pending Kellinger deal instantly became her problem. But as she watched the tall, athletic frame of the other driver, the problem began to look like an opportunity. She re-dialed Dominic, her voice now completely composed—cold steel draped in professionalism.

"Dominic, listen. Daniel is deceased. It's a complete catastrophe for the Kellinger acquisition. The entire fund hinges on replacing his expertise *immediately*," she stated, pacing slightly. "But I have a lead. The man who hit him—Julius Sterling—he was just released from the ER. He's clearly sharp, drives a Honda which means he's likely white-collar but not wealthy, and he was obviously in a highly emotional, vulnerable state. He recently lost his spouse and nearly his life." She paused, letting the implication sink in. "He's distracted, he's bruised, and he's probably facing guilt, whether it's warranted or not. He's the perfect candidate to be..." She sought the right word, a subtle sneer in her tone. "...recruited."

The phone buzzed against Cynthia's ear, Dominic's voice sounding tinny and sharp through the speaker, vibrating with barely contained frustration.

"Recruited?" Dominic snapped. "Cynthia, be realistic. He just killed our star client. The man isn't an asset; he's a liability."

Cynthia paced the length of the hospital corridor, her heels clicking a cold, deliberate rhythm on the linoleum. "He was exonerated on the spot, Dominic. It was a hydroplaning accident—his lane was clear; his speed was legal. The police confirmed every word of his story. He was the victim in that wreckage, not the cause."

She paused, staring through a window at the rain-slicked streets of Detroit below. "He's damaged goods, yes," she continued, her voice dropping to a low, predatory hum. "But he is handsome. He has a presence that you can't teach. And if the rumors about his personal life are right, he's in the middle of a total collapse. He's starting over from zero. He needs money, he needs a sense of purpose, and more than anything, he needs a distraction from his own grief."

She could almost hear Dominic's skeptical frown through the line, but she pressed on, her mind already three moves ahead.

"I'm going to find out where he works—or rather, where he *used* to work. And then I'm going to make him an offer he can't refuse. This isn't just about replacing Daniel, Dominic. It's about finding a new anchor for our clients, the business, and the future. I want someone we can mold from the ground up."

She broke eye contact with the consultation room and moved toward the entrance, grabbing her pristine black coat. "I'll call the investigator right now to get Mr. Sterling's full profile. Every bank statement, every college grade, every job history! Hell, I want to know who he loses his virginity to, I want it ALL!"

"We're here," Jazmine said, her voice softening as she parked the car. "Let's get you inside. You look like a ghost."

The *click* of the deadbolt sliding back was a heavy, final sound. Jazmine pushed the door open to her dark, quiet townhouse.

"Jaz?" someone called out softly.

On the couch, a figure stirred. Mrs. Petrov, Jazmine's neighbor, sat up. An old black and white movie played silently on the TV.

"Hey," Mrs. Petrov whispered, clicking the television's audio down. "You're home."

"We're home," Jazimine said, dropping her purse and keys on the small table by the door. She let out a long, shuddering sigh, the sound of a soldier reaching safety. "Thank God. Home."

Mrs. Petrov stood as Julius shuffled in, his pale, pained face illuminated by the dim lamp. "How is he?"

"He's here. He's okay," Jazmine said, running a hand through her own hair. "Bruised ribs. No breaks. Thank you, thank you for coming on such short notice. How was Leo?"

"Are you kidding? No problem at all," Ms. Diggs said, her eyes fixed on Julius.

"He was a perfect angel, never made a peep.". She turned her full attention to Julius, walking over and giving him a very careful, gentle hug.

"Oh, honey. I'm so glad you're okay. I saw it on the news. It looked... just awful. All that traffic, the lights..."

Julius accepted the hug, his body rigid. "Thanks." He pulled back. "The news... did they... did they give an update? On the other driver?"

Mrs. Petrov's face fell with sympathy. "No, no updates on him. Just a brief recap, said the freeway was partially closed. They did show your car, though." She shook her head. "That bitch is *totaled*."

Julius just nodded. "Yeah. Figured."

She reached over and turned up the volume on the television perched on the counter. Julius leaned in, his bruised ribs protesting the movement, expecting to see a reporter standing in front of the twisted metal of his sedan. Instead, the screen was a chaotic wash of flashing blue lights and yellow crime scene tape.

The news anchor's voice was taut, vibrating with the practiced urgency of a breaking story. *"...reports of a bloodbath at* ***Club Connect****. Early witness accounts suggest a coordinated hit. Two unidentified men in dark coats were seen fleeing the area just as police arrived. At least two confirmed dead, including the club's owner."*

The camera cut to a shaky cell phone video of the club's entrance. Even through the grainy footage, the silence of the alleyway Julius had stood in only an hour ago felt haunted.

"In a related development," the anchor continued, the graphic on the screen switching to a shot of a quiet residential block, *"officers are also on the scene at* ***Seward Street****, where a second shooting has been reported. Neighbors describe hearing multiply shots before a black sedan sped away. Five has been confirmed dead at this location. Police are currently investigating whether these two incidents are linked to a larger turf war."*

Julius felt a cold sweat break across his brow. There was no mention of the hit-and-run that had nearly killed him. No mention of the frantic calls to 911 or the debris on the freeway. His accident—the moment his world had shattered—had been relegated to a footnote, a traffic update buried beneath the weight of a rising body count.

He stared at the screen, his mind racing as the anchor's voice blurred into a drone of tragedy. Seward Street was the location where he got High-Roller's bag.

The realization hit him harder than the airbag ever had, a physical blow that made his lungs seize. The cold, clinical images of Club Connect on the screen weren't just news; they were a tally. Larry. Leon. High-Roller and his people. Folks he had just spoken to, people whose breathing presence was still vivid in his mind, were now just statistics and yellow tape.

"Julius? You look like you've seen a ghost," Mrs. Petrov whispered, her hand trembling as she reached for the remote.

"I have," Julius murmured, his voice sounding hollow, as if it were coming from the bottom of a deep well.

He realized with a terrifying clarity that he was the statistical anomaly. He was standing in that office minutes earlier when the door exploded. He would have been standing at that bar when the silent rounds started flying. Every single person he had interacted with today was dead.

The world wasn't just moving on—it was being torn apart, and the men responsible were moving a lot faster than the police. They were surgical. They were efficient. And they were clearing the board.

Mrs. Petrov glanced at her watch. "Oof. Look at the time. I've gotta run. I have a doctor appointment in the morning."

“Mrs. Petrov, you're a lifesaver. Seriously,” Jazmine said, walking her toward the door.

“Always,” Mrs. Petrov said. take care of each other.”

While Jazmine walked her out, Julius eased himself onto the edge of the couch, every muscle in his body screaming in protest. The front door clicked shut, and the deadbolt slid home. The house fell into a profound, heavy silence.

Rose his hands and covering his face, Julius heard Jazmine in the back hall, the soft *creak* of her Leo's bedroom door opened and closed. She assisted Julius to the spare bedroom. He sat alone, the events of the night crashing over him—Maya, the airbag, the inverted BMW, the blood, the hospital, the police, and now Larry, Leon, T- Booige, and High-Roller. Jazmine re-emerged from the hall carrying a pillow and a folded set of sheets. She placed them on the bed beside him.

“Thanks, sis,” Julius said, his voice thick. “Seriously. For... taking a load off my mind. I didn't even know where I was gonna put my head tonight.”

“Where else would you go?” Jade said softly. She put a hand on his shoulder. “You're my brother, Jay. The spare room is all set. “Get some rest, okay? You look like shit.” She leaned down and kissed the top of his forehead.

“Goodnight.”

“'Night, Jazz.”

He watched her disappear into her own bedroom. He was alone. The only sound was the faint hum of the refrigerator. His eyes found the old mahogany grandfather clock in the corner, the one that had been their mom's.

As if it knew he was watching, the clock began to chime, its deep, resonant bongs filling the quiet house.

Midnight.

One.

Two.

2 AM. The night was finally over once the medication kicked in.

4

Monday morning, Cynthia stepped into her office, the usual rhythm of her routine feeling strangely heavy. She dropped her bag beside her desk with a muffled *thud* and froze. Cynthia received a notification from her laptop. An email with the subject "**CONFIDENTIAL** "was stamped across the line.

Her heart gave a sharp, unsteady skip. She eased into her chair, adjusting her blazer and settling herself with a deliberate breath before opening the electronic mail. With a click of the mousepad, the email opened. She scanned through the summary sheet the investigator provided at the end of the file:

■ Confidential Dossier: Julius H. Sterling (Target: Recruitment)

Prepared for: C. Townsend, Townsend & Associates

Date of Report: 11/06/20XX (07.45 AM EST)

Investigator: Barry, T. (Asset 44)

Subject: Julius Sterling (Involved Party, I-94 Fatality)

I. Biographical & Contact Information

Detail	Finding
Legal Name	Julius Hakeem Sterling

Detail	Finding
DOB/Age	October 15, 2001 (Age 24)
Current Residence	[Address redacted]—Detroit, MI (Leased, unit 402)
Known Affiliation	Jazmine Sterling (Sister, Lives in Royal Oak, MI. Current place of shelter.) Leo Sterling (Nephew, Kid, Lives with mother, Jazmine Sterling, in Royal Oak, MI.)
Relationship Status	Long-term cohabiting partner: Maya Vance. (Complicated)
Vulnerability	High. Appears to be in immediate need of income, shelter, and emotional distraction.

II. Financial Profile (Pressure Points)

Detail	Finding	Notes
Credit Score	615 (Fair)	Score is stable but currently leveraged.
Student Debt	$45,000 (Outstanding)	Federal and private loans. Monthly payments are significant.
Vehicle	2017 Honda Civic (Totaled)	Loss of transportation is a critical pressure point. Insurance claim pending.

Detail	Finding	Notes
Savings	Low liquidity (Estimated < $5,000)	No significant liquid assets or investment portfolios found.
Real Estate	None	Renter only.

III. Employment History

Company	Position	Duration	Notes
OmniTech Solutions	Inventory Support Specialist	5 Years (2021–Present)	Status: Left premises abruptly Friday, 04/05. Unconfirmed termination/resignation. Mid-range salary.
Best Buy	Sales Associate	1 Year (2000–2021)	Entry-level retail.

Key Finding (Employment Exit):

III. Education History

College	Duration	Notes
Michigan State University	4 Years (2016-2000)	Participated in ROTC and Black Cacus. Degree in Information Technology

- Sterling secured an unscheduled exit from OmniTech yesterday (approx. 8:45 PM) by exiting an emergency—claim was "robbery/damage to apartment." This was a premeditated deception to allow him to leave early. Note: This deception was rendered obsolete by the subsequent discovery of his partner's infidelity and the immediate car accident.

- Sterling's therapist, Dr. Alvarez, assisting healthy lifestyle for a condition of 'Depression' and 'Sexual Hypertension' stemming from a traumatic experience in his youth.

IV. Social Media & Character

- Public Profiles: LinkedIn (Professional only, sparse updates). Basic Facebook/Instagram found. Subject maintains a low online profile.
- Character Notes: Consistent employment history over five years suggests loyalty and reliability, contrasting with the desperate action taken Friday. Pending criminal record. Character appears to be highly driven but recently devastated by a significant personal betrayal (confirmed by sister's comments and the scene at his apartment).

Conclusion: Julius Sterling is reliable, educated, and critically, at an emotional and financial nadir. He is in immediate need of a clean slate and redirection, making him highly receptive to a large, life-changing financial offer.

Cynthia reread Barry's report, a slow, satisfied smile spreading across her face. "Julius Hakeem Sterling. Indebted, betrayed, and facing the psychological trauma before and after the accidental death. A clean slate, indeed," she murmured, tapping the profile on her desk. The $45,000 student debt and low liquidity were flashing red flags—flags that spelled opportunity.

It was 8:10 AM. She reached for the phone and buzzed her executive assistant and step-daughter, Carla Preston. "Get Dominic on the line now and clear my schedule until noon…"

Dominic's voice was tight with urgency when he finally picked up, the sound of papers rustling in the background.

"Cynthia, the Kellinger team is panicking," he blurted out. "They're demanding Mrs. Alistair's decision on the financing structure immediately. Did Barry deliver the file, or are we flying blind?"

Cynthia leaned back in her leather chair, the glow of her laptop illuminating a cold triumph in her eyes. "He delivered. And we have our successor. Julius Sterling."

She began to pace, ticking off the details like a grocery list. "Clean record (Before the accident), four years of unwavering loyalty at OmniTech, and currently drowning in financial debt. Better yet, he just walked in on his fiancée—a woman named Maya Vance—in the middle of an affair."

Cynthia paused, savoring the moment. "Yes, Dominic. *Vance.* Daniel's last name. The irony is delicious, don't you think? It's as if the universe is hand-delivering us a replacement."

The silence on the other end of the line stretched a beat too long. Cynthia didn't wait for him to recover. She clicked a pen, her mind already drafting the terms.

"We are moving," she commanded. "I want a draft consulting contract drawn up immediately. One-year term, with an option to extend. Set the base salary at $180,000—that's double what he was making at his old company. But here's the kicker: I want an immediate sign-on bonus of $60,000, paid into a trust account. That wipes his debt clean and gives him a cushion he can't afford to lose."

"That's aggressive, Cynthia," Dominic cautioned, his voice low. "What's the catch? No one signs a deal like that without a hook."

"The catch is total, unquestioning loyalty. And he starts when his signature is on the dotted line," Cynthia replied, her voice hardening. "His official title will be 'Advisor on the Transition of Communication Relations.' In reality, it means he'll be doing exactly what Daniel did, only this time, he'll be under our thumbs."

She paused by the window, watching her reflection. "And Dominic? Make sure the draft includes a binding non-disclosure agreement. It needs to cover the circumstances of his hiring and every detail of the former Daniel's private life. I don't just want his talent. I need control of his story."

Julius sat on the edge of the twin bed in the small, unfamiliar guest room at Jazmine's Dearborn duplex. It was close to eight fifteen in the morning, less than seventy-two hours since his entire life had imploded.

Physically and mentally, he was a total wreck. The prescription painkillers the nurse had pressed into his hand at the hospital were doing little more than rounding off the jagged edges of his suffering; the core of the pain remained untouched. His chest felt as though it had been encased in setting concrete. Beneath the thin fabric of the shirt, a deep, ugly purple-and-red contusion from the seatbelt stretched diagonally across his torso—a violent, throbbing sash that marked him as a survivor. Every breath, no matter how shallow, was a fresh wince, a reminder of the steering column's impact.

The concussion only made things worse, turning the brightly lit room into a dizzying carousel of shadows. He hadn't slept, and he wasn't sure he ever would again. Every time he let his eyelids heavy, the reel began to play: the BMW flipped like a discarded toy, the haunting sight of the man's slack, bleeding face, and then, without transition, the searing image of Maya's desperate, naked pleas in their bedroom.

He was running on nothing but fading adrenaline and lukewarm ginger ale. His mouth felt like it was filled with ash, and a deep, bone-weary fatigue was finally beginning to settle into his marrow. Yet, despite the exhaustion, his mind remained a frantic, buzzing wire that refused to shut off.

The initial volcanic burst of anger and shock had finally cooled, leaving behind a heavy, leaden depression that settled into his very bones. He felt adrift—completely unmoored from his home, his career, and the woman he thought he knew. In the span of a single night, his financial stability and his sense of self had vanished into the Detroit rain.

The heartbreak was eclipsed only by a terrifying numbness. Three years of his life had been revealed as a complete sham; a hollow stage play where he was the only one who didn't know the script. He hadn't just lost a partner; he had lost the entire map of his future. That hollow thud in his chest wasn't just a physical symptom of the crash; it was the sound of a dream dying, and it proved far more agonizing than his cracked ribs.

Then there was the crushing weight of the guilt. The ghost of Friday night that truly haunted him. He kept replaying the seconds before the impact like a film reel stuck on a loop: *Was I slowing down enough? Did I look at the dashboard a second too long?* Though the police had looked him in the eye and cleared him of any wrong-doing, he felt inextricably lashed to the injured man. He felt responsible for the silence in Daniel's home.

For the first time in his adult life, Julius was utterly dependent. He had no car, no liquid assets beyond the crumpled bills in his wallet, and no roof over his head other than the one his sister provided. This newfound vulnerability was a profound humiliation—a jagged pill to swallow for a man who had always defined himself by his iron-clad self-sufficiency.

Cynthia drove toward Daniel's exclusive downtown condo. She needed the keys to his office files. By the time Cynthia parked her car, the initial shock of Daniel Vance's death had solidified into a ruthless, calculated plan to capitalize on the tragedy. She wasn't simply looking for an employee; she was hunting for an asset to secure her own professional future, and she knew the best time to trap a wounded animal was right after the initial injury.

She helped herself into Daniel's apartment, closing the door to hide her visit. She walked around the living room, going straight to his bedroom. Her mind wonder, picturing Daniel and her making love on the different locations of his apartment. Daniel wasn't just for business; he was her pleasure. The hurt of losing him was minor, but strong for losing his existence. She knows his location where a second set of his office keys was: in a firebox located under his bedframe. The key to the firebox was taped behind his mahogany side table leg. She bent down getting the items, unlocking the box. She was receiving a call from Dominic*: "I'll call him right back*" she said to herself.

The keys were on top of his documents: life insurance, savings, Bitcoin investments, etc. Cynthia froze, debating to take the documents and ransack his safe with cash and jewelry.

But Danial's focus on caring and assisting his family sustain a stable and good living echo in her head. She removed the necessity keys from the ring, putting the rest back in the lockbox. One last personal wish that Cynthia can grant to her friend.

She called Dominic back, her voice radiating absolute confidence.

"Forget the Kellinger deal for one minute," Cynthia said, her voice cutting through Dominic's protest like a surgical blade. She paced the length of the plush rug leaving Daniels bedroom, the daylight catching the amber blinds on the window. "Brad Hayes's firm is now handling Daniel's estate, effective immediately. I want our legal team filing the paperwork first thing in the morning."

Dominic's silence on the other end of the line was heavy with calculation.

"I've already consoled Eleanor," she continued, her tone softening into a chillingly rehearsed empathy. "She's completely fragile. She'll defer entirely to me, especially since Daniel was her sole provider. Brad has the time to oversee the portfolio, invest and keep the money flowing for his family for years to come."

"Are you saying..." Dominic paused, the realization dawning on him. "Brad controls his assets and his business dealings now? All of it?"

"I'm saying we control the narrative, Dominic. And more importantly, we control the direction of his portfolio."

Cynthia stopped pacing, her gaze fixing on the city skyline. "That portfolio needs a successor. A fresh face. I want someone with raw talent, someone who hasn't been corrupted by the old way of doing business." Dominic mentioned that the offer sheet was sent to her email. Cynitha walked into the living room where Daniel's printer was. She connected her phone to the printer, printing the offer sheets.

After getting off the phone with Dominic, she gathers the documents, grabbed her purse, throwing her coat over her arm. Exiting the apartment, she walked to her black Mercedes S-Class. The next location was to Jazmine Sterling's address, pulled directly from Barry's report.

She drove, applying a single layer of rich crimson lipstick in the rearview mirror. This wasn't a job interview; this was a rescue mission draped in corporate luxury. She needed to approach Julius while the memory of the betrayal and the sound of the crash were still raw.

Pulling up to the modest, well-kept duplex, she checked the time: 10:15 AM. Perfect. She wasn't just offering him a job; she was offering him an escape route out of grief and debt. Cynthia stepped out of the Mercedes, her designer heels clicking lightly on the pavement. She carried a sleek, embossed leather briefcase containing the contract and a checkbook. *She wasn't just recruiting an analyst; she was recruiting a future asset, and the* ***price was exactly $60,000 and a clean conscience upfront.***

Julius heard the ***clicks*** of the expensive heels, a sound that sliced through the thick silence of the house, followed by a light but authoritative knock on the front door.

Downstairs, Jazmine glanced at the clock—10:18 AM—and frowned. She wasn't expecting anyone. She quickly wiped her hands on a towel and headed toward the entrance, her expression tightening with suspicion. Jazmine pulled the door open and stopped dead.

Standing on her small porch was a woman who looked like a hallucination from a different world. Cynthia exuded the kind of polished, ruthless power that screamed of downtown high-rises and closed-door board meetings. She was dressed in a sleek black suit, a coat draped with effortless precision over her arm, and a stunningly embossed leather briefcase held in a manicured hand.

"Yes?" Jazmine's voice was laced with immediate suspicion. "Can I help you?"

"Good morning. I apologize for the unannounced visit." Cynthia offered a smooth, professional smile, though her eyes were already busy, subtly assessing the modest interior of the duplex. "I'm Cynthia Townsend. I'm looking for a Mr. Julius Sterling. I understand he's staying here with family."

The protective barrier went up instantly. Jazmine squared her shoulders, physically blocking the view into the house. "Who are you? And how do you know where he lives? He just got out of the hospital."

Cynthia didn't flinch. She kept her tone low, expertly blending professional concern with a veneer of practiced sympathy.

"I know, and that is precisely why I'm here. I represent the family of Mr. Daniel Vance—the other driver involved in the accident last night."

She saw Jazmine flinch and quickly gestured to her briefcase. "I assure you; I am not here to accuse anyone. I am here strictly on business, to offer Mr. Sterling a substantial professional opportunity that, given the circumstances, I believe he desperately needs."

The blood drained from Jazmine's face. "Mr. Vance's family? He... he died, didn't he?" The weight of the fatality hit her all over again. "Look, my brother is in rough shape. Physically and emotionally. He's not seeing anyone, especially not people involved in that tragedy."

Cynthia leaned in slightly, dropping her voice to a confidential, magnetic murmur. "Jazmine, is it? I understand your impulse to protect him, but please understand mine. I'm a director and an executive. I know what happens when someone leaves a traumatic scene with severe debt. The guilt can destroy a man. This isn't about the crash; it's about giving him a massive, immediate financial solution to his problems. A clean slate, as it were."

The mention of a "clean slate"—and the chilling realization that this stranger knew about Julius's financial vulnerability—startled Jazmine.

"A job offer?" Jazmine hesitated, a flicker of calculation finally crossing her eyes. "He just... he just survived a wreck. Besides, he already has a job."

"A significant, life-changing career offer," Cynthia countered, seizing the opening with the precision of a predator. "Please, just give me five minutes. This is urgent, and I promise you; this meeting could be the only good thing to come out of Friday night."

The low hum of the argument had reached the upstairs bedroom. Julius slowly pushed himself upright, his bruised chest screaming in protest as he forced his lungs to expand. He shuffled to the top of the stairs, his knuckles white as he gripped the railing for support.

"Jazz?" his voice was weak and hoarse, barely carrying down the hall. "Who is it?"

Jazmine turned, looking from her broken, hollowed-out brother to the flawlessly composed woman on her porch. The silence stretched for a moment before she finally stepped aside, swinging the door wide.

"It's for you, Julius," Jazmine said, her voice resigned. "I think you need to hear what she has to say."

Jazmine stepped aside, her body stiff with a resentment she couldn't quite name. Cynthia didn't wait for an invitation; seizing the slight opening, she moved past the threshold with the practiced ease of someone who always belonged exactly where she stood. She looked up the stairs at Julius, her gaze a perfectly calibrated mixture of professional gravitas and deep-seated, rehearsed sympathy.

"Mr. Sterling," Cynthia said, her voice dropping to a smooth, confidential register, as if the very walls of the duplex had ears. "I know this timing is inappropriate. But I'm going to be direct, and I need you to understand that what I am offering must remain strictly between us."

Julius descended the last three steps slowly, his hand white-knuckled on the railing. The pain in his ribs had shifted from a sharp bite to a dull, constant fire. He stopped on the final step, towering slightly over Cynthia, yet in the presence of her focused intensity, he felt infinitely smaller.

"What are you talking about?" Julius asked, his voice a hoarse rasp. "My sister is right here."

Cynthia ignored the comment, her focus absolute. "I represent the business interests of Daniel Vance. His death has created a massive, immediate leadership vacuum in the community relations department for the City of Detroit—handling sensitive, high-value assets. We need an intelligent, trustworthy anchor immediately."

She snapped open her sleek briefcase and withdrew a crisp, multi-page contract. "Your sister is right; you need to hear this. But," she added, her eyes cutting toward Jazmine, "she does not need to know the price."

Cynthia moved past Jazmine and laid the briefcase flat on the small kitchen table. When Jazmine took a confused step toward them, Cynthia preempted her with a sharp, quiet command.

"Ms. Sterling, I will need your brother's full attention for five minutes. Perhaps you could get him a glass of water?"

The demand was so imperious that Jazmine bristled, her mouth opening to protest, but the sheer coldness in Cynthia's eyes made her hesitate. Julius, too numb to care about the breach in etiquette, simply watched. As Jazmine turned toward the sink, Cynthia leaned in close to him. Her expensive perfume enveloped him, a scent of high-end department stores and cold silk.

"Mr. Sterling—Julius—I know everything," she whispered, her voice a conspiratorial hum. "I know about the forty-five thousand in student debt. I know you have no savings. And I know you left work early Friday because your girlfriend, Maya Vance, was sleeping with another man."

Julius felt the air leave his lungs in a sharp, involuntary hiss. Cynthia didn't flinch; she let the silence confirm her intelligence.

"The woman cheating on you shares the same last name as the man who died in that accident," Cynthia continued. "The man I represent. This is your secret, Julius, but in my hands, it is also your leverage."

The blood drained from Julius's face. The physical shock of her words eclipsed the fire in his ribs. The connection—the name *Vance*—hit him like a second collision. *How does she know?* he wondered wildly. *The debt? The name?*

"How... how do you know all that?" he whispered, horrified.

Cynthia smiled faintly, tapping the contract with a manicured nail. "I have my sources. What matters is that I am offering you a way out. A way to silence the guilt, pay the debt, and never look back."

She flipped the contract to the second page, her finger landing on the bolded figures. "A one-year consulting contract. A hundred-and eighty-thousand-dollar salary PLUS incentives. And to ensure your absolute loyalty regarding the private affairs, an immediate sign-on bonus of sixty thousand dollars."

She pulled a checkbook from the briefcase. A check was already filled out, sitting there like a trap or a lifeline, waiting only for his name.

"That pays the debt. It replaces your car. It gives you a safety net you've never had," she said, her eyes locked onto his hollow ones. "All you have to do is take the job, start tomorrow, and never tell a soul—especially your sister—why I truly hired you. This is your clean slate, Julius. Your chance to make Friday night disappear."

Julius felt a wave of visceral, sickening shock, yet beneath it was a terrifying lack of surprise. The figure—the sixty thousand to buy his silence—felt less like an ethical breach and more like the standard cost of doing business in a world he didn't understand. He looked at the high-end check, then back at Cynthia's cold eyes.

He had seen the BMW on the highway. He had seen the designer suit on the man in the wreckage. He knew, subconsciously, that the people who lived in that world didn't leave things to chance. They executed profiles. They bought outcomes. They erased mistakes.

"Maya Vance..." Julius managed a slow, painful shake of his head. "She has the same last name..."

"A detail that is irrelevant," Cynthia whispered, leaning closer still, "provided it stays out of the media. What matters is that you have nothing to go back to and nowhere to go. And I have the only solution you're ever going to get."

He swallowed hard, the bitterness of his failure mixing with the dizzying allure of the paper in front of him. It wasn't a career move. It was a contracted oblivion, and as he looked at the check, he realized he was already halfway to signing his life away.

Jazmine returned from the sink, the glass of water trembling slightly in her hand. She set it down on the table with a sharp *clack*, her eyes darting between the thick legal document and the predatory stillness of the woman sitting in her kitchen.

"A consulting contract?" Jazmine asked, her voice tight with skepticism. "For what, exactly? My brother is an inventory specialist for a tech company. What does he know about 'private investment portfolios' for people?"

Cynthia didn't even look up, her gaze remained fixed on Julius, though she addressed Jazmine with a cool, dismissive politeness. "The portfolio requires someone with a background in crisis management and clear internal communication. Your brother's track record at OmniTech is exemplary in that regard."

Julius, however, wasn't buying the corporate jargon. He leaned heavily against the table, his ribs throbbing in time with the pounding in his head. "Jazz is right," he rasped, his eyes scanning the staggering figures on the page again. "I'm an analyst, Cynthia. I don't move millions of dollars around. Why me? Why am I suddenly 'qualified' to step into a dead man's shoes?"

Cynthia's expression didn't soften, but her eyes sharpened, turning into chips of flint. "You're qualified because you are a blank slate with a high IQ and a desperate need for a new life. You're qualified because you have no ties to the vultures currently circling our clients. I don't need a financial genius; I have a floor full of those. I need a man who owes me his entire existence. I need someone who understands the value of *discretion* because his own secrets are just as heavy as the ones he'll be guarding."

She looked at him with a terrifying clarity. "You aren't being hired for what you know, Julius. You're being hired for who you are—and more importantly, for what you've survived."

Before Julius could respond, Cynthia's wrist flicked upward. She checked her thin, diamond-encrusted watch, her brow furrowing slightly.

"It's nearly eleven," she murmured, more to herself than them. The atmosphere in the room shifted instantly; the focused, personal intensity vanished, replaced by a cold, executive briskness. She stood up, smoothing the front of her black suit coat. "I have a twelve thirty appointment at the Fisher Building that cannot be moved."

"Wait—you can't just drop this and leave," Jazmine protested, gesturing at the checkbook still sitting on the laminate table.

"I've said what needs to be said." Cynthia slid the check into the breast pocket of Julius's wrinkled t-shirt—a gesture that felt both intimate and territorial. She tucked the contract back into her briefcase with a series of efficient clicks. "I apologize again for the suddenness of the offer, and for the intrusion. Truly."

She walked toward the door, her heels clicking a sharp, final rhythm against the floor. At the threshold, she paused and looked back at Julius. The warmth was gone. It was purely a matter of business now.

“The clock is ticking, Julius. You have till Friday night to put your name above the dotted line. After that, the trust account is dissolved, the check is voided, and I find someone else to fill that seat. If you want to disappear from the mess your life has become, this is the only way out.”

She stepped out into the gray Detroit morning, the door closing behind her with a soft, decisive click. The silence that followed was deafening. The scent of her expensive perfume lingered in the small kitchen, clashing with the smell of Jazmine’s laundry detergent and the stale air of a house in mourning. Julius stood frozen, his hand pressed against the pocket where the sixty-thousand-dollar lifeline sat against his bruised skin. She turned slowly; her eyes fixed on the pocket of Julius’s shirt where the check sat. “Julius,” she whispered, her voice cracking. “What the fuck just happened? Who *is* that woman?”

Julius didn't answer immediately. He sank into a kitchen chair, the movement sending a fresh jolt of agony through his torso. He reached into his pocket and pulled out the check, laying it flat on the table. The zeros seemed to vibrate under the fluorescent light.

“She’s a lifeline, Jazz,” he rasped, staring at his own name written in perfect, calligraphic ink. “Or a noose. I can’t tell yet.”

Jazmine moved toward him, her protective instincts flaring back to life. “She knew things, Julius. She knew about the debt. She knew about... the girl.” She paused, her voice softening. “Maya Vance”.

Julius closed his eyes, leaning his head back. The image of the bedroom door swinging open flashed behind his lids. He let out a jagged, self-deprecating laugh that turned into a wince. "The man I hit... Daniel Vance. He was her brother, Jazz. Or a cousin. Or a husband. I don't know. But the coincidence is what she's buying. She's buying my silence so the 'Vance' name doesn't end up in a scandal or something."

"Sixty thousand dollars is a lot of money for silence," Jazmine said, pulling out the chair opposite him. "And a hundred and eighty thousand a year? Julius, people don't give that kind of money to inventory workers from OmniTech. They give that money to people they want to own."

"I'm already owned!" Julius suddenly snapped, his voice rising before breaking into a cough. He gestured vaguely at his bruised body and the small house. "I have forty-five thousand dollars in debt hanging over my head. My car is a scrap heap on I-94. My bank account is a joke. I'm have a hospital bill coming for that damn accident. And the woman I was going to marry is... she's gone. I have nothing, Jazz. I am a ghost standing in your kitchen."

Jazmine reached across the table, covering his shaking hand with hers. "You have me. You have Leo. You have a home here as long as you need it."

"I can't be a burden to you," he whispered, looking at her with hollow eyes. "You're working double shifts just to keep the lights on for you and Leo. And now I'm here, a broken wreck eating your food and taking up your guest room." He looked back at the check. "This pays you back. It pays for Leo's school. It wipes the slate."

“At what cost?” Jazmine asked, her eyes searching his. “She looked at you like you were a piece of property she was acquiring, Julius. Not a person. If you take that money, you’re working for the people associated with the man you... with the accident. How are you going to wake up every morning and walk into that office?”

Julius looked down at the check, his thumb brushing the signature. The physical pain in his ribs was nothing compared to the void where his life used to be.

“I don't think I have to worry about waking up, Jazz,” he said quietly. “I haven't really been asleep since I saw that BMW flip. I think I’m just waiting for the world to start moving again. And she’s the only one offering a shove.”

He looked at the calendar. Four days. The countdown had already begun.

5

The Wednesday morning air was crisp, but every breath Julius took sent a sharp, reminder-throb through his bruised ribs—the lingering souvenir from the accident. He shifted carefully in the passenger seat of Jazmine's car, wincing as the seatbelt retracted against his chest.

"You sure you're ready for this?" Jazz asked, her hands gripping the steering wheel. She idled at the curb, looking at him with deep concern. "You still look like you went twelve rounds with a semi-truck."

"I need the hours, Jazz. And I need to get my mind off the accident," Julius said, checking his reflection in the visor mirror. The cuts on his forehead and the right side of his face were scabbing over, angry red lines against his skin, but the swelling had finally gone down. "Thanks for the ride. I'll call you before I get off from work."

"Be careful, Jay."

He stepped out, watching her drive away before turning toward the looming gray factory. A knot of anxiety tightened in his stomach, distinct from the physical pain. *Heaven knows I'm about to get grilled,* he thought. Craig, the shift supervisor, didn't believe in accidents. Julius had taken unscheduled days off—time he didn't have to spend—and he knew Craig was likely sharpening his knife at that very moment, waiting to carve him up for it.

Inside, the familiar hum of the conveyor belts and the acrid smell of hydraulic fluid hit him. He made his way to his station, moving a little stiffer than usual.

"Yo! Thought you quit on us!" one of the loaders shouted over the noise. Julius managed a grin, raising a hand.

"Nah, just needed a break."

"Man, what happened to your face?" another asked, squinting at the healing cuts.

"Rough weekend," Julius deflected. By the looks of things, the rumor mill hadn't caught up yet. They didn't know he had been involved in the crash; they just seemed glad he was back to pull his weight. For a moment, the normalcy felt good. He logged into his computer to check his email, ignoring the twinge in his side, and got to work.

An hour into the shift, the rhythm of the job almost lulled him into a sense of security. Then, he felt a tap on his shoulder. He turned to find Karen, the building's HR specialist. Usually, she carried a clipboard and a forced corporate smile, but today her hands hung limp by her sides. She looked down at her shoes before dragging her gaze up to meet his.

"Julius?"

"Yeah? Sorry I wasn't here the last couple of days, but I have a doctor note. Is everything alright?" he asked, wiping his eyes from staring at the screen. A sorrowful expression washed over her face, her eyebrows knitting together in genuine distress. She ignored his question.

"You need to report to the main office," she said, her voice barely audibles over the machinery. She added a soft, pained, "Please."

Julius's stomach dropped. *Here we go,* he thought. *Craig's going to write me up for the absence.* He walked the long concrete hallway to the office, steeling himself for a lecture on attendance policies. But when he opened the door, the atmosphere wasn't administrative; it was suffocating. It wasn't just Craig.

Detective Diaz, a man Julius recognized from the chaotic blur of the accident scene, stood on one side of the entrance. Next to him was his partner, Officer Krupke, a burly uniformed cop, and a young, slim officer standing rigid near the door whose name tag read Jefferson. Craig was seated behind Karen's desk, legs crossed, looking comfortable. Too comfortable. A smirk played on his lips, the kind of look a man gets when he has a secret he's dying to share.

Julius stopped in the center of the room. "What's going on?" he asked, trying to keep his voice steady, though his eyes darted between Craig's smug face and the Detective's grim expression.

"Julius," Detective Diaz said, his voice flat and professional. Then, he spoke the words Julius had feared since the tires screeched that night. "You're under arrest."

The room seemed to tilt. Officer Krupke stepped up behind him, reaching for the handcuffs on his belt. The metal clicked ominously.

"Arrest?" Julius stammered, pulling his wrist away instinctively before Krupke grabbed it firmly. "Arrest on what charge?"

"Manslaughter," Diaz said. He didn't blink. "The man you were involved with in the accident Saturday died. We were just waiting on the warrant to come pick you up."

The air left Julius's lungs. *Manslaughter.* The word echoed in his skull. He felt the cold steel ratcheting tight around his wrists, pinching the skin.

"You have the right to remain silent," Krupke began, droning out the Miranda rights as he guided Julius toward the door.

"Hold on," Craig interrupted, his voice slicing through the tension like a serrated blade. He stood up, smoothing his tie. "Officer, just a moment." He looked at Julius, that smirk widening into a sneer. "Since you're being HAULED OFF, I should inform you that this company has a zero-tolerance policy regarding criminal conduct. That, included with your unexcused absence... your employment here has been terminated. Effective immediately."

Julius stopped. The shock of the arrest momentarily gave way to a white-hot heat rising from his damaged chest. He looked at Craig—at the satisfaction in the man's eyes. The smell of the office—stale coffee and Craig's cheap, overpowering cologne—burned Julius's nostrils. It felt personal. It felt evil. His soul burned with rage. The fear evaporated, replaced by four days of pain and anxiety exploding all at once.

"You know what, Craig?" Julius shouted, spinning around despite Krupke's grip. "You sorry, miserable son of a bitch!"

"Easy," Krupke warned, tightening his hold.

"No!" Julius roared. He unleashed a torrent of expletives, attacking Craig's character and the way he looked down on everyone. The office workers in the cubicles outside stood up, heads popping up like gophers, staring as Julius was shoved toward the door. "I should had fucked your daughter when I had the chance, you crusty-faced bastard!"

Craig's smirk faltered, replaced by shock, but Julius was already being hauled into the hallway.

As the adrenaline faded, the reality rushed back in. He was in handcuffs. He was being walked down the main corridor. *Manslaughter.* He realized with a sinking heart that he couldn't say anything to prove his innocence. Not here. Not now. He saw the double doors leading to the main factory floor ahead—the "walk of shame" in front of the entire shift.

"Wait," Julius pleaded, planting his feet. He looked at Detective Diaz. "Please. Don't take me through the plant. Don't let them see me like this."

The detectives exchanged a glance. Diaz looked at the young officer, then at Krupke. They weighed the request. Suddenly, the door to the admin supply room opened and Vanessa stepped out. She froze, seeing Julius in cuffs. Her hand flew to her mouth.

"Is there another way out?" Diaz asked her.

Vanessa blinked, tears welling in her eyes as she looked at her best work friend. "Y-yes," she stammered, pointing down a side corridor. "You can take the back door around the corner. That directs you right to the parking lot."

"Thank you, miss," Diaz said. He nudged Julius toward the side hall. Vanessa caught Julius's eye as he passed. Her face was a mask of sadness, a silent goodbye. Julius couldn't bear to look at her. He kept his face solid, staring straight ahead, his jaw clenched tight to keep his lip from trembling.

Inside, his internal organs felt like they were melting with fear and embarrassment. His life was unraveling in real-time. They pushed through the heavy steel exit door and the bright sunlight hit him; blinding compared to the dim hallway. They walked him to the waiting patrol car.

As Krupke opened the back door, pushing Julius's head down to clear the frame, Julius spoke, his voice quiet now. Broken. "Can I call my sister? When we get to the precinct?"

"After you get booked," Krupke stated flatly, shoving him into the hard plastic seat. "You'll get your phone call then."

The door slammed shut, sealing Julius inside with nothing but his thoughts and the wire mesh separating him from his freedom.

The fluorescent lights overhead hummed with a rhythmic, headache-inducing buzz. Julius stared at his fingertips, where the ink from the fingerprint pad sat tacky and black, staining his skin like a permanent mark of shame.

Snap.

The camera flash exploded in his vision, leaving white spots dancing in the dark. In that fraction of a second, the lowest moment of his life was digitized and filed away for the state's archives.

"Move it," an officer grunted, gripping Julius's elbow.

The air grew thick as they descended toward the holding cells, a suffocating cocktail of industrial bleach, unwashed bodies, and the metallic tang of old fear. When the heavy iron door groaned open, Julius's stomach twisted into a hard knot. The men inside looked as though they had been forged by the very rebar and concrete that held them.

He was scared as hell, but he forced his features into a mask of stone. He couldn't look like a punk. Not here. Scanning the hellish space, he spotted a sliver of privacy—a tiny gap at the front corner of a concrete bench, right against the bars. He strolled toward it, carefully mimicking the heavy, careless gait of the men around him. When he sat, the cold steel bit into his back through his thin shirt. He was packed in so tight with the others they were practically exchanging DNA.

Time didn't just pass; it dragged like a heavy chain. The silence was punctuated only by the low, guttural groans of a man in the back and the sharp, predatory whispers of two inmates plotting in the shadows. Julius stared at the floor, his heart hammering against his ribs.

Two hours in that piss-hole felt like an eternity. Finally, an officer approached the gate, his keys jangling like a death knell.

"Sterling!" he barked.

The bars slid open just wide enough for Julius to squeeze through. The officer pointed toward a wall-mounted phone. "One call. Make it quick."

Julius's fingers trembled as he punched in the only number he had left in the world. He held his breath through the rings. One. Two. Three.

"Hi, you've reached Jazmine. Leave a message..."

His heart plummeted. "Jazz, it's me," he whispered, his voice cracking as he leaned into the plastic receiver. "I'm in jail. I need you to come get me. Please... I'm at the 2nd precinct. Just... please hurry."

He hung up and looked at the officer, but the man didn't return the gaze. He was too busy scribbling on a clipboard. "This way."

The chain between Julius's cuffed hands clinked with every step. He was led into a desolate interrogation room. "Wait here," the guard said, gesturing to the center of the room. The door clicked shut, the sound echoing like a gunshot. Julius sat on a cold metal chair, shaped so unnaturally it felt designed to paralyze. Small windows, caged in by rusted mesh, filtered in a sliver of dismal gray light. The walls were dingy, covered in paint chips that sprinkled the floor like snow—years of witnessed confessions flaking into the dust.

He stared at the locked door, the detective's earlier words ringing in his ears like a siren. *Murder*. The realization hit him with the force of the car accident itself. That meant the man he hit—Daniel Vance—was dead. Julius's chest heaved. The air in the room felt too thin to support life. He leaned forward, resting his forehead against the freezing metal of the table, and realized the worst day of his life had just found a way to get darker.

He closed his eyes and whispered a desperate prayer. He hasn't been a deeply religious man since his years in catholic school. But right now, God was the only one who knew the truth of what had happened in that rain. A sharp knock rattled the door.

A scrawny, dorky-looking man walked in with a folder tucked under his arm. He was older, with hair combed aggressively to the side and glasses that seemed too large for his head. His suit looked like a desperate find from a thrift store.

Is this the man supposed to defend me? Julius thought, his stomach sinking further. *I'm doomed.*

"I'm Stewart Washington, your court-appointed counsel," the man said, his voice as thin as his frame.

Julius gave him a skeptical side-eye, letting out a low, defeated, "Okay."

"Whatever you do," the lawyer whispered, leaning in, "don't say a word until I tell you to. Deal?"

Julius took a deep breath, surrendering his well-being to a man who looked like he couldn't win a traffic dispute. But before he could process his doom, another knock jumped him nearly out of his skin.

The woman who walked in was à stark contrast to the gloom of the precinct. She was slim with a rich mocha complexion, her hair styled perfectly with a soft fringe over one eye. She wore a fitted black suit that commanded attention, radiating a mixture of confidence and high-end authority. Despite the handcuffs and the murder charge, Julius felt a primal stir of distraction; her presence was a sudden, electric jolt to his system.

"I'm Lauren Cooper," she announced.

A female officer entered behind her, standing guard at the door. Julius's lawyer looked up, then at Julius, and abruptly snapped his folder shut.

"Tell her anything and everything," the lawyer said. He stood up and headed for the door.

"WTF?" Julius hissed under his breath. He expected his lawyer to stay, to guide him, to be his shield. Instead, the man was leaving him high and dry.

Ms. Cooper sat down, her expression unreadable. The conversation that followed was brief and terrifying. She laid out the details of his arrest and the mountain of trouble he was facing. She made it clear: she was his only chance.

"All you have to do is follow my lead," she said, her voice smooth but firm. "Accept everything without question. My boss will explain the details to you later."

"Can I talk to my sister about this?" Julius asked, glancing at the door.

Ms. Cooper's eyes snapped from her paperwork to his. "No. Once I walk out that door, the offer is gone. And so is your freedom."

Julius felt utterly defeated. He was out of options and out of time. "I'll follow your lead," he whispered.

A smirk played on her lips—a look that felt more predatory than professional. "Well, give me a moment while I work my magic."

She gathered her things and disappeared. Left alone in the quiet, Julius's mind raced. He thought of his freedom, his family, and the sheer, terrifying weight of the situation. His leg shook with a nervous energy he couldn't suppress. He put his head back down on the table, exhausted by the sheer gravity of the unknown.

Minutes later, the door swung open again. Ms. Cooper returned with the officer.

"Release him," she commanded. She looked at Julius, a small glint of triumph in her eyes. "And you don't need to call your sister. She's already in the lobby."

Julius's eyes widened. The officer stepped forward and unlocked the cuffs. The sudden lightness of his wrists felt foreign.

"Follow me," the officer said.

Julius walked through the station, his heart leaping as he saw Jazmine sitting in the lobby, her face tight with worry.

"Jazz!" he called out.

She stood up, her eyes flooding with relief, and met him with open arms. As they embraced, Julius felt a hand grip his arm. He turned to see Ms. Cooper standing there, her expression chillingly calm.

"You're free to go," she said, her voice low. "My boss will be in touch soon to discuss... everything."

She let go of his arm and stepped back, that same devilish smirk returning to her face. Julius shivered. He was free, but as he walked out of the station into the cool air, he realized he was now beholden to a power he didn't understand.

Jazmine held Julius tightly in the precinct lobby, her hug a desperate attempt to anchor him back to reality. When she finally stepped back, her face was a map of exhaustion, fear, and protective rage.

"Oh, Julius, thank God!" she managed, her voice thick and trembling. She gripped his hand, pulling him toward the heavy glass exit doors. "Are you okay? What in God's name happened? I was at work when you called—I thought it was a prank at first. Then I called back and they said you were being booked for *manslaughter*—"

She cut herself off, noticing the duty officer's cold, watchful eyes following their every move.

"We need to get out of here," she hissed, pushing him through the doors and into the cool, quiet safety of the night. Julius didn't answer. He just kept walking, feeling the invisible weight of the "magic" from Ms. Cooper had worked, wondering exactly what it was going to cost him.

Once they were settled in Jazmine's car, the silence was heavy, punctuated only by Julius's uneven, shallow breathing. Jazmine's hands shook as she fumbled with the keys to start the engine.

"Okay. Start talking. Slowly," she commanded, her eyes fixed on the windshield. "Did they charge you? Why manslaughter? The officer at the scene said it was an accident, pure hydroplaning! And who was that woman? The one who looked like she stepped off a magazine cover—she said she got you released. Who is she, Julius?"

Julius rubbed his bruised temples, his mind racing to construct a story. He had to explain the arrest, his firing, and this sudden release without mentioning Cynthia's blackmail or the dark underbelly of Daniel Vance's business.

"It's worse than an accident, Jazz," he said, his voice flat and hollow. "They arrested me because I was on the phone, distracted. They called it 'culpable negligence.' They booked me and fired me on the spot."

Jazmine's knuckles turned chalky as she clutched the steering wheel. "Oh, Julius. Oh my God. You were right to be scared."

"And the woman... her name is Lauren Cooper," Julius continued, the lie tasting like residue in his mouth.

"She's a lawyer, an executive who worked with Cynthia. She saw the whole situation—the debt, the cheating..." He stumbled, unable to say Maya's name clearly. "...the mess I'm in."

He took a ragged breath. "She made me an offer Monday, Jazz. A huge job. A consulting role, big money. I turned it down earlier because it felt too weird. But when I got arrested, I had no choice. She must have called the DA or someone high up. She got me out, but I have to accept the deal."

Jazmine stared at him in disbelief. "She bought you out of jail? Just like that? Julius, that's insane. That's not legal."

"I don't care," he snapped, the desperation leaking through his mask. "I'm unemployed, I have nothing, and I was looking at a cage. She told me the job is the only way to make the case go away."

Jazmine watched him, the raw pain in his eyes contradicting the fantastic nature of his story. She knew he was hiding something huge, but the fact remained: he was free.

"Okay," she whispered, pulling out onto the road. "We'll deal with this. We'll deal with Cynthia and her devil deals when you're thinking straight. For now, you're coming home and you are not leaving that house until we know what is going on."

The car ride toward the duplex was a blur of streetlights and shadows, but inside the quiet cabin, the gears in Julius's mind began to grind. He stared out the passenger window, watching the city's grime pass by, as Lauren Cooper's parting words replayed in his head like a looped recording.

"My boss will explain the details to you later."

The realization didn't hit him all at once; it seeped in, cold and oily. He remembered the way Lauren had walked into that interrogation room—the predatory confidence, the way the dorky court-appointed lawyer had folded like a cheap suit the second she appeared. No mere lawyer had that kind of gravity. She was a messenger.

Cynthia.

The name felt like a bruise in his mind. Julius's breath hitched, and he squeezed his eyes shut. He put two and two together, and the sum was a death sentence to his dignity.

Lauren wasn't just a high-level lawyer; she was the scalpel Cynthia Townsend used to cut through red tape. The "magic" hadn't been a legal miracle or a stroke of luck—it had been a purchase.

"Julius? You're shaking," Jazmine said, her voice tight with concern as she navigated a turn. "What is it?"

"Nothing," he lied, his voice sounding thin and brittle to his own ears. "Just the adrenaline wearing off."

But inside, his stomach was a riot of nausea. He realized with terrifying clarity that the bars of the holding cell hadn't actually disappeared; they had just expanded to encompass his entire life. Cynthia hadn't just sent a lawyer to help a "friend"—she had reached into the bowels of the precinct, plucked him out of the state's hands, and placed him firmly in her pocket.

The weight of it made it hard to swallow. Every time Lauren had said *"Accept everything without question,"* she was really saying *"You belong to her now."*

He looked down at his hands, still stained with the faint, grey residue of fingerprint ink. He felt a sudden, desperate urge to scrub his skin raw. He wasn't a free man being driven home by his sister; he was a piece of collateral being transported to a new owner.

6

When Jazmine finally pulled into the driveway of the duplex, the familiar sight of the peeling paint and the sagging porch offered no comfort. It looked like a trap. As he stepped out of the car, the humid night air felt heavy, pressing against his chest. He knew that the moment he stepped inside, the phone would ring. He knew that the "boss" Lauren mentioned wasn't going to offer him the job again—she was going to issue a command.

He looked at Jazmine, who was watching him with wide, hopeful eyes, and he felt a wave of profound self-loathing. She thought the nightmare was ending. He knew it was only moving into a more expensive room. While Jazmine drove toward the safety of the duplex, the true "magic" was being settled in a private office back at the station.

"Captain," Ms. Cooper said, leaning across the desk with steely intent. "Daniel Vance was a discreet client of my close circle. We understand you are pursuing a manslaughter charge, but we know the crash was caused by hydroplaning. We have zero interest in dragging the private affairs of Mr. Vance's associates through a long, costly trial."

Captain Rodriguez looked skeptical. "The state still has a case, Lauren. The driver admitted distraction."

"What I am offering is closure," Ms. Cooper countered. "My people have secured Mr. Sterling a highly remunerative, private position with a wealthy client—a position that requires absolute discretion and loyalty. We will not oppose a non-custodial bond, provided he immediately reports to this employer."

She leaned in closer, her expression ice-cold. "His freedom is tied directly to his new service contract."

The heavy glass door of the captain's office swung open with a sharp click that cut through the precinct's hum. He emerged with his jacket off and sleeves rolled up, looking less like a man in charge and more like a man looking for an exit.

He marched straight toward the desk shared by Diaz and Krupke, his expression unreadable until he was standing directly over their cluttered workspace. He leaned forward, pinning a thin manila folder to the desk with the weight of his palm.

"Vance case is officially off your plates," he said, his voice dropping to a low, pragmatic tone. "The third precinct is taking lead so I need everything you have on my desk by the end of y'all shift."

Krupke started to protest, but the captain held up a hand to silence him. "It's not a knock on your work. This isn't about performance. The forensics coming back suggest this is tied to a specific, high-level situation the Feds have been tracking for months. It's out of our jurisdiction now."

Seeing a politically smooth way out of a complex case, the captain had already greased the wheels of the handoff. He agreed to a **Personal Recognizance Bond**, effectively washing the department's hands of the immediate fallout. In the quiet of the holding area, Lauren signed the paperwork—her signature a final, steady seal on Julius's new life.

The oppressive weight of the moonlighted beat down on the windshield as Jazmine pulled the car into the concrete driveway. The engine cut out, leaving a sudden, ringing silence that felt heavier than the noise it replaced. She didn't move immediately; instead, she gripped the steering wheel, her eyes fixed on the peeling paint of the duplex.

"The house will be quiet," Jazmine murmured, finally turning to look at Julius. Her voice was soft, thick with an exhausted kind of empathy. "I'm glad Leo is spending the night at my friend Sarah's house. He's only a child, Julius. He doesn't need to see his uncle looking like this—broken down and looking over his shoulder."

Julius stared out the side window, his reflection ghostly against the glass. He looked fragile, his skin sallow in the harsh light.

"You need the peace anyway," she continued, reaching over to briefly squeeze his hand. Her palm was warm, a stark contrast to the cold dread pooling in his stomach. "You can't heal if you're constantly trying to put on a brave face for a seven-year-old. I'm going back to work and give you some space to just... breathe."

She sighed, a sound that seemed to carry the weight of the entire week. "Take the time, Julius. Please. Just rest."

The tires crunched over the dry pavement, kicking up a thin veil of dust as Jazmine backed out of the driveway. Julius stood motionless on the porch, his shadow stretching long and thin against the front door. He watched the glint of the street light hit her side-view mirror until the car disappeared around the corner, leaving him in a sudden, unsettling silence.

The air around the duplex smelled of freshly cut grass and the faint, acrid scent of distant car exhaust. It was a normal, suburban night, but to Julius, the atmosphere felt charged and heavy. He felt the profound, terrifying isolation of the empty house looming behind him—a hollow space where he was meant to "rest."

He knew the peace Jazmine had promised was a luxury he couldn't afford. Between the shadow Cynthia cast over his life and the news of a faceless arrest looming on the television, the quiet wasn't a sanctuary; it was a cage. He crossed the threshold into the living room, the familiar scent of lemon wax and old carpet doing nothing to soothe the terrifying confusion about his "employment."

The pain and the guilt were overwhelming while turning on the TV. He was trapped—not by iron jail bars, but by a gilded cage forged from his own debt and Maya's betrayal. He knew one thing with absolute certainty: Cynthia owned him. The peace of the duplex allowed Julius the needed rest on Jazmine's couch. It took less than an hour before the peace was shattered by the sharp, demanding ring from his cell phone, a sound that grated against the bare walls. Julius froze, his breath catching in his throat as his heart hammered painfully against his bruised ribs. The vibration seemed to rattle his very bones. He didn't need to check his broken screen; he knew the cold precision of that rhythm. It was her.

"Hello?" he croaked into the receiver, his voice sounding thin and foreign in the empty room.

"Julius," Cynthia's voice drifted through the line, cool and entirely devoid of warmth. "Good. You are free because I personally assured the captain you have secured immediate, stable employment. The terms of your release are now fully dependent on you fulfilling that obligation."

The room felt smaller, the air thicker. "The sixty thousand..." he managed, his voice trembling with a mix of hope and terror. "When does that clear?"

"The funds will clear the moment the signed contracts are returned," she said, her tone indifferent to the sheer desperation bleeding out of him. "They will be deposited into a new account. That money is for your debt and a new vehicle. Your full salary is paid upon successful completion of your service requirements in partially payments."

She paused, and Julius could almost feel her predatory gaze through the phone line. "But we aren't doing this over a computer screen, Julius. A digital signature is too impersonal for a commitment of this magnitude."

A chill crawled up his spine, settling in his marrow. "What do you mean?"

Across the room, the television screen flickered with a breaking news bulletin. The bold banner at the bottom caught his eye: ***ARREST MADE IN VANCE HOMICIDE***. The anchor's voice was a low murmur, stating that an individual was finally in custody for the death of the beloved Daniel Vance. However, the report offered no names, no faces, and no details—just the haunting fact that someone was behind bars.

"I mean tomorrow we will be going to Daniels's funeral, "Cynthia said, her voice sharpening.

"I've already picked out a suit for you; Just wash your ass and get the suit when I get there by nine"

The air left Julius's lungs as if he'd been punched. He stared at the TV, at the faceless announcement of an arrest, and felt the walls closing in. "Cynthia, I can't," he hissed, his eyes wide with panic. "The news... they just said they have someone in custody for Daniel's death. They haven't said who it is yet. If I show up there while everyone is looking for a killer to hate, it's a death sentence for my reputation—if not my legal case."

"On the contrary," she replied, her voice smoothing out like polished silk over a blade. "The fact that they haven't named the suspect is exactly why you're going. Showing up with me makes you look grieving and supportive. It paints you as a mourner, not a monster. Besides, Julius..."

There was a terrifying finality in her tone, the kind that left no room for negotiation or dignity. "We both know you don't really have a choice in where you go anymore. Wash up, get the suit, and accompany me."

The line clicked shut with a sharp, mechanical finality, leaving him in a silence far more deafening than the ringing had been. Julius stared at his phone for a heartbeat before sliding it onto his front pocket. The next morning, He walked into the cramped bathroom, the air smelling of shampoo and freshly washed towels. Shoving his sleeves up and splashed cold water onto his face, desperate to wash away the sallow, haunted look in his eyes.

With trembling fingers, Julius began to strip off his wrinkled clothes, the sterile white light of the bathroom humming overhead like a warning siren. He scrubbed his skin until it was raw, his breath coming in jagged hitches.

His hands were shaking. He scrambled down the stairs, his chest tight, and cracked open the front door. There, idling like a predatory shark against the curb, was Cynthia's sleek black sedan. Julius didn't make eye contact with the tinted windows. He simply reached into the back seat as the door electronically clicked open, retrieving a heavy, high-end garment bag. The fabric felt expensive—too expensive for a man in his position.

Back inside, the clock on the wall seemed to tick with the force of a hammer. Julius looked at the garment bag hanging on the door hook in his room. The news had said someone was in custody for Daniel's death—a faceless, nameless suspect. As he fumbled with the zipper of the suit, a sickening thought crossed his mind: *If the public doesn't know who is in custody, they'll be looking for someone to blame at that funeral. And I'm walking right into the center of it.*

Julius stepped out of the duplex, the charcoal-grey suit fitting him with a precision that felt more like armor than clothing. The fabric was stiff and smelled faintly of dry-cleaning chemicals and Cynthia's expensive, floral perfume. As he descended the porch steps, the humid afternoon air pressed against him, making the silk lining of the jacket feel like a suffocating second skin.

Cynthia was leaning over the passenger seat of the sedan, her sunglasses reflecting the suburban street like twin obsidian mirrors. She didn't say a word; she simply gestured toward the door with a flick of her wrist. Julius climbed in, the leather seat cool against his back, and the car glided away from the curb in a predatory, electric silence.

The drive to the church was a blur of grey pavement and flickering shadows. When they finally pulled up to the curb, the sight made Julius's stomach turn. A sea of black umbrellas and somber overcoats spilled out from the stone archway of the Woodward Cathedral. News vans were parked down the block, their long antennae reaching toward the overcast sky like skeletal fingers.

"Remember," Cynthia whispered, her voice a silk thread as she adjusted his lapel. "You are the support of a grieving friend. Nothing more, nothing less."

The curb was a chaotic swarm of flashing lights and shouting voices. As the black town car pulled to a stop, Cynthia was immediately engulfed by a sea of reporters. Microphones, wrapped in foam and bearing news station logos, thrust toward her face like reaching hands.

"Cynthia! Over here!" a reporter yelled over the engine noise. "How are you handling the loss of a colleague so close to the department?"

Cynthia paused, her expression a mask of practiced, somber grace. She looked directly into the nearest lens, her voice steady despite the visible shimmer of grief in her eyes. "Loss is never easy," she began, "but when it is someone who shared your daily life, your coffee, and your triumphs, it leaves a void that words can't quite fill."

"And what about Mr. Vance's legacy?" another journalist pressed. "What did he mean to this city?"

Cynthia took a shallow breath, her hand tightening on her clutch. "Mr. Vance wasn't just a pillar of the community; he was its heartbeat. He believed in the potential of these streets when others had given up. The city feels quieter today because a giant has fallen."

A few yards away, Julius stepped out of the car, his legs feeling like lead. The reporters' voices faded into a dull, underwater hum as he focused on the looming structure ahead. Every step toward the heavy oak doors felt like a descent into something final.

As he crossed the threshold, the world of buzzing cameras and city grit vanished. The air changed instantly—the natural warmth of the afternoon sun was replaced by the stale, refrigerated chill of the narthex. It was a cold that didn't just touch the skin; it seemed to settle in the bone.

Then, the scent hit him. It was the cloying, overwhelming fragrance of hundreds of lilies, thick enough to taste. The floral sweetness felt aggressive, a forced beauty meant to mask the reality of the polished casket waiting in the shadows of the sanctuary. Julius kept his eyes down, the rhythmic click of his dress shoes on the marble floor the only sound he could bear to hear.

The muffled sound of an organ groaned from the loft, a low, mournful vibration that rattled in Julius's chest. Heads began to turn. He felt the weight of a hundred gazes—some filled with pity, others sharp with a suspicion that made his skin crawl. He kept his eyes fixed on the flickering prayer candles at the front of the aisle, his heart hammering a frantic rhythm against his ribs. Somewhere in this room, people believed a killer had been caught, and yet here he was, walking through the center of their grief.

Julius felt like a ghost walking among the living. Every step toward the open casket felt like dragging weights. When he finally looked down, his stomach turned. Daniel looked waxen, his features frozen in a peace he hadn't known in his final moments. Julius felt a sickening cocktail of guilt and resentment—this man was the reason his life was currently in shambles, yet here he was, paying respects under duress.

"He looks smaller than I remembered," Cynthia whispered, her hand firm on Julius's elbow, guiding him like a handler.

As they turned away from the casket, Julius's heart stopped. Standing near the floral arrangements was Maya. She looked beautiful in her mourning veil, but she wasn't alone. Clinging to her arm was the man she had cheated on Julius with—the man who had shattered his world long before the legal system tried to finish the job.

The heavy silence of the service shattered the moment the pallbearers slid Daniel's polished mahogany casket into the back of the black hearse. As the crowd began to drift toward their parked cars for the procession, Julius saw her. Maya was standing near the curb; her hand tucked firmly into the crook of another man's arm.

The anger was instantaneous, hot and sharp, searing through the fog of Julius's grief. He broke away from Cynthia's side, his feet moving with a lethal purpose before his mind could catch up.

As the crowd trickled out toward the line of waiting cars, Julius pulled his coat tight, tucking his chin and moving behind a group of grieving relatives. He wanted to be a ghost—to pay his respects and vanish before the reality of the situation imploded. But his efforts were useless. Amidst the sea of dark wool and somber faces, Maya stood like a beacon of accusation. Her eyes locked onto him with a sharp, sudden clarity that made his breath hitch.

"Julius?" her voice rang out, brittle and sharp enough to stop him in his tracks. "What are you doing here?"

Julius froze, his attempt at anonymity crumbling. He slowly turned to face her, but his gaze didn't stay on Maya for long. It drifted to the man standing beside her. Despite the thick, low-hanging clouds that threatened rain, the man wore a pair of heavy, designer sunglasses. They sat awkwardly on the bridge of his nose, clearly intended to mask the jagged, purple-yellow bruising of the black eye Julius had delivered only days prior. The man shifted uncomfortably, a muscle in his jaw leaping, but he remained silent behind his dark lenses. But before the newcomer could utter a word, a shadow fell over the trio, cold and imposing.

Cynthia stepped into the circle, the sharp scent of her expensive perfume cutting through the cloying smell of the funeral lilies. She didn't spare a single glance at Maya or her companion. Instead, she placed a steadying, possessive hand on Julius's arm, her gaze lingering on his face with an intimacy that felt scandalous in the presence of the dead.

"Is there a problem, darling?" Cynthia asked. She slid her arm through Julius's, her fingers moving slowly, deliberately, until they were intricately tangled with his. She leaned her head slightly toward his shoulder, the picture of a woman claiming her territory.

Maya blinked, her face flushed with a mix of confusion and sudden jealousy. "Who are you?"

"I'm Cynthia," she said, her voice dropping into a sultry, proprietary register. "I was Daniel's boss. I'm also the one Julius is with now." She squeezed his hand, giving the space the unmistakable impression that their bond was far deeper than professional. "We have to go, Julius. We can't be late for the procession to the cemetery."

She turned to Maya with a chillingly polite smile. "It was so lovely to see Julius's... acquaintances. Come, Julius."

As they walked toward the car, Daniel's mother approached them, her eyes red-rimmed. She grabbed Cynthia's hands. "Thank you, Cynthia. Thank you for paying for everything. I don't know what we would have done."

"It was the least I could do for such a devoted employee," Cynthia said softly, her face a mask of perfect sympathy.

The cemetery was a sea of grey stones and damp grass. The air was biting, and the sound of the casket being lowered into the earth was a final, jarring thud. As the crowd began to disperse, drifting away in small, somber groups, Cynthia led Julius down a winding path toward the iron gates.

"You handled that woman pretty damn well," Cynthia remarked, her heels clicking on the stone path. "Though I suspect my intervention helped."

“Why did you do that?” Julius asked, his voice exhausted. “The hand-holding, the ‘darling’... you made it look like I’m your property.”

“In a way, you are,” she replied casually. “But let’s talk business. You’ve seen what I can provide—protection, status, a way out. How do you feel about your new ‘escort’ profession now that you’ve had a taste of the elite?”

Julius looked out at the rolling hills of the graveyard. “I feel like I’m trading one prison for another. And Lauren Cooper? Getting me out on bail was a miracle, but I know she didn’t do it for charity.”

“Lauren does what I tell her to do,” Cynthia said. “As for what’s in it for you? Freedom from a cell. A life of luxury. All you have to do is accept that your life belongs to the business. You have just over twenty-four hours to make a final decision on my offer, Julius. Don't waste them.”

She stopped at the gate, turning to face him.

“Tomorrow night, Thomas Morris Museum” she said, smoothing the lapel of his suit.

“I expect you to be there. Consider it your debut.”

They stepped into her waiting car, leaving Daniel’s family mingling in the cold silence of the dead. Cynthia leaned back against the hand-stitched leather of the seat, her silhouette sharp against the passing city lights.

"It’s a black-tie affair—strictly exclusive," she said, her voice smooth and deliberate. "I will be attending, of course, and you will be coming as my guest. It’s time you saw the world from the inside."

She turned her head slightly, her gaze catching his. "I'll bring the physical contract with me to the event, but a copy was sent to your email. We will sign the documents together, in person, before you are officially introduced to the circles you now serve. Consider it your initiation."

The thought of a gala, of lights and people and pretending to be someone he wasn't, made his stomach churn. Cynthia continued "I will provide the driver and he will be at your door at seven sharp. In the truck is a second suit for you to wear as well. Julius, your responsibilities are simple: ensure you are healthy and well-rested, and prepare yourself to accept the opportunity of a lifetime."

The car glided to a halt in front of the duplex, the engine's expensive purr a sharp contrast to the cracked pavement and the fading afternoon light of the neighborhood. Julius felt a heavy, sinking sensation in his chest—a strange vertigo that came from being caught between Cynthia's polished world and the grit of his own reality. With a soft *thud*, the trunk popped open. Cynthia didn't move to get out, nor did she look back. She simply waited, her profile silhouetted against the windshield like a statue.

Julius stepped out, his dress shoes crunching on the gravel that had washed onto the sidewalk. He walked to the rear of the vehicle, where the trunk lid stood open like a hungry mouth. Resting inside was the garment bag—a sleek, midnight-black sheath that held the tuxedo. As he lifted it out, the weight of the fabric felt significant, almost like a suit of armor he wasn't sure he was worthy to wear. It smelled of cedar and high-end boutiques, a scent that felt entirely foreign in the humid, stagnant air of the block.

He gripped the hanger tightly, the plastic digging into his palm. With a firm shove, he slammed the trunk shut. The sound echoed down the quiet street, a final, metallic punctuation mark on their conversation.

Without a word or a wave, Cynthia pressed the accelerator. The car surged forward, its tires kicking up a fine, gray veil of dust that swirled around Julius's ankles. He stood there on the curb, the garment bag clutched against his chest, watching the red glow of her taillights vanish around the corner. The silence that followed was deafening, leaving him alone in the settling dust with a life he no longer recognized.

Entering through the door, Julius felt the walls of the kitchen closing in. He looked toward the hallway, knowing Jazmine was just in the other room, thinking he was safe. He was anything but safe. He was a bird being told how to groom its feathers before being put on display.

Julius darted to the guest room, laying the garment on the bed and scrambled to the small, dusty laptop Jazmine kept on the desk. He logged into his email, his hands shaking so violently he struggled to type the password. The encrypted file was there, sitting in his inbox like a coiled snake—the digital copy of what he would be signing in ink the following night.

He downloaded the contract and began to skim. The figures were astronomical: **$180,000 Annual Retainer Fee. $60,000 Signing Bonus.** It was an escape from his poverty, but the "Scope of Work" was a nightmare of vagueness: *"The contractor agrees to provide personal, discreet, and highly tailored availability... ensuring unwavering loyalty and emotional support as required by the client."*

Julius retreated to the bathroom and splashed cold water on his face, staring into the cracked mirror. This was supposed to be his time of recovery. He had been working so hard to manage the hypersexual urges that had plagued him since the trauma of his youth—the "beast" that he had tried to cage with discipline and therapy. Now, he could feel the cage door rattling.

The stress of the manslaughter charge, the crushing weight of the debt, and now the explicit nature of Cynthia's "service" was like pouring gasoline on a flickering ember. His heart rate spiked, not just from fear, but from a dark, involuntary anticipation. The hypersexuality was a coping mechanism, a physiological response to trauma that he had been fighting to unlearn. But Cynthia wasn't asking him to heal; she was paying him to relapse.

"I can't do this," he whispered to his reflection. "It's going to kill me."

"Julius?" Jazmine's voice called out from the hallway, soft and filled with worry. "Are you okay in there?

"Yeah, Jazz," he lied, his voice cracking as he looked into the mirror. "I'm just... I'm just exhausted."

He stood up straight, trying to force the tension out of his shoulders. He felt a wave of profound self-loathing. Cynthia wasn't just buying his time; she was buying the very part of him he was desperate to fix. He walked out of the bathroom, his mind already drifting toward the black-tie event, feeling the "beast" in his mind wake up, fed by terror and the gilded promise of a life that would never let him heal. Julius retreated to the guest room, the shadows stretching long across the floorboards. Every time he closed his eyes, he saw the flash of the precinct camera or the cold, predatory smirk on Lauren Cooper's face.

His skin felt electric, a restless, buzzing heat beneath the surface that made his muscles twitch. The "beast" was pacing the cage of his mind, fed by the high-stakes terror of the last few hours.

Desperate to drown out the internal noise, Julius reached into his old pants pocket and pulled out his earphones. His fingers fumbling, a slight tremor still present in his hands. He settled onto the edge of the bed, the mattress sighing beneath his weight, and pushed the buds into his ears. He scrolled through his phone until he found a slow, melodic jazz playlist. As the first notes of a mournful saxophone drifted through the speakers, the sharp edges of the room seemed to soften. The bass was a steady, rhythmic pulse—a substitute for the frantic hammering of his own heart.

He lay back, staring up at the darkened ceiling where a sliver of moonlight filtered through the blinds. The music was a silken veil, wrapping around his consciousness and shielding him from the reality of the contract, the debt, and the hotel room waiting for him in the near future. For a few minutes, he wasn't a man owned by the state or someone working for the city; he was just a soul drifting in the blue notes of a trumpet.

Slowly, the tension began to drain from his jaw. The music acted as a temporary sedative, numbing the hypersexual thrumming in his veins just enough to let his exhaustion take over. With the smooth, brassy wail of the jazz as his only companion, Julius finally felt his eyelids grow heavy. His breathing deepened, and he slipped into a fitful, shallow sleep, the rhythm of the music guiding him down into the dark.

7

The Thomas Morris Museum of African American History loomed against the Detroit skyline, a striking fortress of modern glass and solemn brick. Outside, the Friday night air carried a sharp, refreshing chill, but inside, the Ford Freedom Rotunda was alive with a warm, pulsing energy.

It was a cathedral of light and ambition. Above them, the massive glass dome acted as a dark mirror to the city's night sky, while the floor—inlaid with the intricate "Genealogy" map—felt like hallowed ground beneath Julius's polished shoes. The air was a cocktail of expensive cologne, aged scotch, and the soft, rhythmic hum of a cello quartet.

Julius adjusted the cuffs of his new tuxedo, the heavy silk feeling like a second skin. He felt like an imposter in a kingdom of giants until he saw a face that grounded him in a reality, he thought he'd left at the curb of the duplex. Across the sprawling circle of the rotunda, standing near the towering African masks, was Chris.

He wasn't draped in the bespoke luxury that Cynthia's guests wore; his tuxedo was a rental, slightly boxy in the shoulders, but he held a glass of champagne with a familiar, easy confidence. Julius felt a jolt of pure adrenaline—part surprise, part dread.

"Chris?" Julius murmured, the name catching in his throat.

Chris turned at the sound of his name, his eyes widening behind his fake glasses. A slow, knowing grin spread across his face as he sauntered over, weaving through the clusters of city council members and CEOs.

"My man, Julius! Look at you," Chris said, whistling low as he took in the razor-sharp cut of Julius's suit. "Man, I heard you were moving up, but I didn't know you'd climbed all the way to the muthafucka penthouse."

"What are you doing here, Chris? This isn't exactly the Friday night spot for the you."

Chris laughed, taking a slow sip of his drink. "Perks of the new gig, man. After you left, I was promoted to yo spot! OmniTech became a 'Bronze Sponsor' for the museum's education wing. They had an extra seat at the table because Craig punk ass caught the flu. I put my hand up before the email even hit the muthafucka inboxes. I figured, why should some old fuck have all the fun?"

The weight of the garment bag he'd carried from Cynthia's trunk suddenly felt heavy again, even though the suit was now on his back.

"Check the ratio, Julius. Look at all this brain food we're about to feast on." Julius forced a smile, though his eyes scanned the crowd with a guarded weariness. He had thrown on a dark Henley, hoping the shadows of the gallery would mask the exhaustion etched into his face—exhaustion that reached down to his very marrow.

The first floor was bustling. A DJ set up near the expansive circular floor was blending classic R&B and Afrobeats at a tasteful volume. Julius felt the low thrum of the bass vibrating in his chest, and for a terrifying second, the rhythm magnified the ghostly, aching pain in his bruised ribs.

Get out of your head, he commanded himself. *Just look at the art.*

They drifted toward the permanent exhibition, *And Still We Rise.* Chris, usually the king of distractions, actually stopped to read a plaque detailing the Middle Passage.

"Hold up, Julius. This is deep," Chris murmured, his playful energy momentarily subdued. "Like, really deep."

Julius leaned in, his eyes tracing the stark descriptions of the slave trade. The weight of generational struggle and resilience chronicled on the walls was immense—a pressure of history so vast it almost dwarfed his own immediate, self-inflicted crisis.

"Yeah, man. This is why I mess with museums," Julius said, a genuine note finally breaking through his fatigue. "It's a different kind of therapy."

They moved deeper into the galleries, pausing beneath the Tuskegee Airmen exhibit. A brilliantly restored PT-13D Stearman biplane trainer hung overhead, a soaring symbol of achievement in the face of systemic hatred. Julius stared at the pilot's helmet displayed under the glass. *Defying the odds. Proving your worth.* The words hit him like a physical blow. He was a man who had a good job, a sister who loved him, and a nephew who looked up to him—and he had nearly traded it all for a moment of reckless negligence.

A waiter drifted by, holding a silver tray laden with fine wine. Julius and Chris each took a glass, the cool stem of the crystal feeling foreign in Julius's hand.

"Imagine being told you can't fly, then you're flying the plane protecting the bombers," Chris whistled, impressed. He turned, catching the haunted look in Julius's eyes. "What are you thinking about, G? You look like you just saw Kobe."

Julius shook his head quickly, taking a sharp sip of the wine. "Nothing. Just… thinking about how easy it is to mess things up. How one wrong move can undo all that hustle."

"Nah, man. The Airmen didn't crash and give up. They kept flying," Chris said, clapping him on the back. He hit a sore spot, and Julius winced, his face contorting in a brief flash of pain. "Look, I got an idea. Let's head to the sports gallery. They got Ali's gear. That'll cheer you up."

In the sports exhibit, Chris immediately started posing next to a life-sized photo of Muhammad Ali. "This is where the smart chicks are, Julius! They love a brother who appreciates history and can quote a couple of Ali's rhymes."

Julius nodded, but his mind was elsewhere. Across the rotunda, a woman was making her move. Clad in a sleek, shimmering dress, she introduced herself to Chris, her sudden, melodic laugh puncturing the hum of the crowd as she played along with his jokes. He tried to engage, tried to feel normal, but the anxiety was a constant, low-grade fever under his skin. His relationship was in ashes, a man was dead, and the fragile peace of the museum was starting to crack. He wanted to run, but he couldn't go home—not until he faced the choice Cynthia had laid out for him.

He attempted to slip away before the night's main applause had even died down. The hallway lights felt too aggressive, the laughter too loud. He moved without thinking, his keys cold between his fingers, ducking into a side stairwell. It was a place with no witnesses and no expectations.

"And where do you think you're going?"

The voice was sweet, but it had a spicy, commanding edge that stopped him mid-step.

Julius turned to see Cynthia. She was stunning, her hair perfectly coiffed, wearing a black dress with a daring slit that showcased the line of her thigh. She radiated power and effortless beauty, making the volcano in my pants swell.

"I was… I just needed to leave the area," Julius stammered, his heart racing. "Too much going on in there."

She laughed, a melodic sound that didn't quite reach her predatory eyes. She walked over and slid her arm under his, pulling him close. "Usually, they do that to a person. Let's go somewhere quiet. We have some things to talk about anyway."

She guided him out of the museum and onto the street. Walking down Warren Avenue toward Brush Street, Julius felt entirely out of his comfort zone. It wasn't the dim streetlights or the fear of the neighborhood; it was the fact that Cynthia was a titan in this city. Every few minutes, they were stopped. People asked where she was going or congratulated her on a recent contract for the city.

To the world, she was a leader. To Julius, she was the woman currently tightening the noose around his neck. The cool night air of the Cultural Center did little to soothe the heat rising in Julius's chest. As they walked, the rhythmic *clack-clack* of Cynthia's heels on the pavement sounded like a countdown. She held his arm with a proprietary grip, her silk sleeve brushing against his skin, a constant reminder of the tether between them.

"You look stiff, Julius," Cynthia said, her voice cutting through the distant hum of traffic. "You should be celebrating. Most men spend their entire lives praying for a doorway to open. I've practically unhinged the gate for you."

Julius looked at the passing shadows of the brick buildings, feeling the eyes of every passerby. "It's hard to celebrate when I feel like I'm walking to gallows," he muttered.

Cynthia stopped abruptly under the orange glow of a streetlamp on Brush Street. She turned to him, her mocha skin glowing, her expression shifting from playful to razor-sharp. "Gallows? You're walking toward a six-figure salary and a clean record. Do you have any idea how many people I've had to silence to keep your name out of the morning headlines?"

"I know," Julius said, his voice dropping to a hoarse whisper. "I know what you did. But this job... replacing Vance... it's not just 'consulting,' is it?"

Cynthia didn't answer immediately. She simply smiled—that same devilish smirk he'd seen before—and began walking again, pulling him along. "We're here."

They stopped in front of a nondescript; heavy oak door tucked into the side of a refurbished warehouse. There was no sign, only a small brass plaque that caught the light. When they stepped inside, the atmosphere shifted instantly. The bar was a sanctuary of dark mahogany, amber lighting, and the expensive scent of aged bourbon and expensive perfume. It was a place for people who didn't want to be found unless they wanted to be seen by the right eyes.

The bartender, an older man with silver hair and a vest, gave Cynthia a knowing nod. She led Julius to a secluded booth in the far back, shielded by a high velvet curtain.

"Two Old Fashioneds," she commanded without looking at a menu.

As they sat, Cynthia reached into her designer clutch and pulled out a slim, leather-bound folder. She laid it on the polished wood table between them like a challenge.

"This is the physical copy, Julius," she said, her voice low and intimate, barely rising above the soft jazz playing over the speakers. "The digital world is for business. This... this is for us. This is the pact."

Julius stared at the folder. The weight of the museum's history—the Tuskegee Airmen, the struggle of the Middle Passage—felt miles away now. He thought about the plane hanging from the ceiling, the symbol of fighting for a freedom that was always being denied. Here he was, about to sign his own away.

"You said I'm replacing Daniel," Julius said, his pulse thrumming in his throat. "What exactly did he do for these 'principals'?"

Cynthia leaned forward, the slit in her dress falling away to reveal the elegance of her legs, her scent—something like vanilla and cold steel—filling his senses.

"He provided what they couldn't buy at board meetings and ground breakings, Julius. Peace of mind. Discretion. A certain kind of... attentive company that understands the value of a secret." She tapped the folder. "Tonight, you sign. Tomorrow, you meet Mrs. Alistair. You'll find that when you have enough money in the bank, the 'shame' you're feeling right now starts to feel a lot like luxury."

The waiter arrived with the drinks. Julius grabbed his glass, the cold condensation stinging his palm, and took a long, burning swallow. He looked at Cynthia, whose eyes were fixed on him, waiting for his surrender.

"Sign it," she whispered. "And let the beast out of the cage, Julius. It's the only way you're going to survive this."

The amber light of the booth felt like a spotlight as Cynthia slid a heavy, gold-plated fountain pen across the table. It came to rest atop the leather folder, a silent invitation to seal his fate.

Julius stared at the document. The legalese seemed to blur, but the figures stood out in sharp, unforgiving black ink: **$180,000**. It was enough to wipe away his debt, to provide for Jazmine and Leo, to finally stop the drowning sensation he had felt for years. But as he looked at the pen, his stomach did a slow, nauseating roll.

"You're overthinking it again," Cynthia said, her voice a soft purr. She leaned back, crossing her legs, the silk of her dress rustling in the quiet alcove. "In ten minutes, that weight on your chest? That fear of the police, the fear of the bank? It all vanishes. All you have to do is write your name."

Julius reached out, his fingers brushing the cold metal of the pen. "And if I want out? In six months? A year?"

Cynthia's smile didn't fade, but it grew colder, more clinical. "The contract is clear, Julius. You stay until the service is complete, or you stay in a cell. There is no middle ground in the world I'm bringing you into. We value loyalty above all else. Because loyalty is the only thing that keeps the secrets safe."

He thought of the museum—the Tuskegee Airmen who had fought for a country that didn't love them back. He felt like a traitor to their legacy, selling the very agency they had bled to secure. But then he thought of the holding cell. He thought of the smell of bleach and unwashed bodies, and the sound of the iron door groaning shut. His hand trembled as he flipped to the final page. The line for his signature looked like a jagged scar waiting to be filled.

"For Leo," he whispered to himself, the thought of his nephew being the only thing that kept his heart from failing.

He uncapped the pen. The nib was sharp, the ink flowing easily as he pressed it to the paper. *Julius…Julius Sterling.* He watched the wet ink catch the light before it soaked into the fiber of the page, binding him to the city of Detroit residents—and to the whims of the woman sitting across from him.

Cynthia reached out and took the folder back the second he finished. She didn't even look at the signature; she just tucked it into her clutch with a satisfied snap of the magnet.

"Welcome to the inner circle, Julius," she said, raising her glass in a mock toast. "Drink up. You have a big night tomorrow. I'll have Carla send the details for the Wellington Hotel. Don't be late. Mrs. Alistair isn't a woman who enjoys waiting. But tonight, you can relax."

Julius drained his glass, the bourbon burning a path down his throat, but he couldn't get rid of the chill. He felt hollowed out, like a shell of a man. He had bought his freedom, but as he looked at Cynthia's triumphant expression, he realized he had never been more of a prisoner in his life.

The amber glow of the booth seemed to deepen as the second round of drinks arrived. The initial tension had bled into a strange, heavy intimacy. For an hour, the "Director" mask slipped, and they spoke not of contracts or accidents, but of the ghosts of their pasts.

Cynthia spoke of a childhood in Boston-Edison area where the cold was a constant companion and the expectations were higher than the skyscrapers. Julius told her about his up bringing on the Westside of Detroit. About the weight of being the man of the house too young, and the quiet pressure of Jazmine's hopes. For a moment, they weren't master and servant; they were just two people who had clawed their way out of the dirt.

Cynthia swirled a glass of Old Fashioneds, her eyes fixed on Julius with a predatory curiosity.

"You have a fire in you, Julius," she whispered, her voice like velvet. "But it isn't natural. It's scorched earth. Tell me—who started the fire? How was this beast inside you created?"

Julius looked down at his hands, his knuckles still faintly aching from the weekend's violence. The shadows of the room seemed to pull the memory from him. "It wasn't a slow burn," he began, his voice raspy and thick with a decade of buried shame. "It was an execution."

He leaned back, the leather creaking under his weight. "I was six. Just a kid trying to find his way in a world that felt too big. My parents hired her as my sitter, three times my elder. She had this way of looking at me like I wasn't a child, went hand to hand with the responsibility I was handling.

Cynthia watched him, her expression unreadable.

"I didn't just let her in; I had a mad crush on her," Julius said, a bitter laugh escaping his throat. "The bar was dark, smelling of stale beer and cheap perfume. We sat in a booth in the back, away from the neon lights. She spoke about life and power as if she owned both. When she touched my hand, I felt like I was being knighted. I didn't see the trap until the door was already locked."

He closed his eyes, seeing the flicker of the bar's dim lamps. "She took my innocence that night and other nights, right there in the back room. It wasn't love. It was a lesson. She used me to feel powerful and then she discarded me like a used cigarette. She broke the part of me that believed people were inherently good. When I walked out of that room, I wasn't a boy anymore. I was hollow. And that hollowness... that's where the beast crawled in to sleep."

Cynthia reached out, her fingers grazing his jaw, cold and sharp. "She didn't break you, Julius. She pruned you. She cut away the soft parts so the iron could grow."

Julius looked up at her, the pain in his eyes hardening into something jagged. "Is that what we're doing tonight? More pruning?"

"Tonight," Cynthia said, a slow, dark smile spreading across her face, "we give the beast a throne."

As the night matured, the bottle of bourbon between them grew lighter. Cynthia leaned her head back against the velvet, her eyes lidded. When she finally stood to leave, she swayed just a fraction of an inch.

"I think," she murmured, clutching her bag, "that the road would be a very dangerous place for me to navigate right now."

Julius stood quickly, instinctively reaching out to steady her by the elbow. Her skin was warm, the contact sending a jolt through his nerves. "I'll call your driver; you should be safe in valet. He can take us to your place. I don't want to explain to Dominic why you're stumbling through the front door."

Cynthia let out a sharp, dry laugh. "Dominic? My driver went home an hour ago—something about a sick kid. And Dominic isn't my husband, Julius. He's a partner in our open relationship. A business arrangement that shares a roof."

Julius frowned, his mind hazy from the alcohol. "Then let me drive us to your place."

Cynthia turned on him, her eyes flashing with a sudden, sharp clarity despite the drink. "You? You've been drinking as much as I have. Imagine the headlines, Julius: *'City Director's Car Pulled Over After Hitting Innocent Bystander.'* It would be on the news before my head hit the pillow. My career would be ashes by sunrise."

The gravity of the situation settled over him. "Then what? We can't stay here in the bar."

"I was expected to stay downtown anyway," she said, smoothing her dress over her hips. "The Wellington is two blocks away; we can sleep it off there!" She looked at him, her gaze traveling up from his shoes to his eyes, lingering on his mouth. "You're escorting me. I'm not walking those streets in these heels alone."

They stepped out into the night. The city felt different now—vibrant and predatory. Julius stayed close, his arm hovering behind her back as they navigated the sidewalk toward the historic Wellington Hotel. The grand stone facade of the building loomed over them, a relic of old-world Detroit luxury.

As they entered the lobby—all gold leaf, hushed whispers, and marble—the reality of the situation hit Julius. He felt the "beast" in his mind stirring, fueled by the bourbon and the scent of her perfume.

"I'll get you to your door," Julius said, his voice hoarse.

Cynthia checked in with a flick of a black credit card, the clerk not daring to ask questions. As they moved toward the elevators, she glanced at him, a mischievous, dangerous glint in her eyes.

"Don't look so terrified, Julius," she whispered as the elevator doors slid shut, sealing them in the small, mirrored space. "I won't bite. Unless, of course, you want me to."

The elevator ascended in a stomach-flipping rush. Julius stared at his reflection—the dark Henley, the bruised face, the man who had just signed his life away. Beside him, the most powerful woman he had ever met leaned against the railing, waiting to see exactly what kind of man she had bought.

The elevator doors slid open with a soft, muted chime, revealing a hallway lined with plush, crimson carpeting that swallowed the sound of their footsteps. Cynthia led the way, her gait slightly more rhythmic and looser than it had been at the museum. Julius followed, his heart hammering a frantic rhythm against his ribs. The air in the hallway was cool, smelling of expensive wax and lilies, but he felt as though he were walking into an oven.

She stopped at a heavy mahogany door and swiped the key card. The lock clicked—a sharp, final sound—and she pushed the door open. The suite was a sprawling display of Gilded Age opulence. Floor-to-ceiling windows offered a jagged, glittering view of the Detroit skyline, the city lights shimmering like fallen stars. A velvet sofa sat in the center of the room, and the air carried the faint, lingering scent of lavender.

Cynthia kicked off her heels the moment the door thudded shut behind them. She sighed, a sound of pure, unadulterated relief, and tossed her clutch onto a side table. "God, my feet were screaming," she murmured.

Julius stayed by the door, his hands shoved deep into the pockets of his Henley. The room felt too small, despite its grandeur. "You're safe. I should... I should probably call that Uber now," he said, though he didn't move.

Cynthia turned around, her hair slightly tousled, her eyes dark and heavy with the bourbon they'd shared. She walked toward him, the silk of her dress whispering against her legs. She stopped just inches away, close enough that he could feel the heat radiating off her skin.

"You're so eager to run back to that duplex, Jay. May I call you, Jay?" she said, her voice dropping to a low, melodic vibration. "Is it the guilt? Or are you just afraid of what happens when you aren't hiding behind a steering wheel?"

"I'm not afraid," Julius lied, his voice cracking.

"Liars are so tedious," she whispered. She reached up, her fingers cool and steady as she traced the line of his jaw, lingering near the bruise he'd earned during his arrest. "You have that look in your eyes. A hunger that you try so hard to pretend isn't there."

The "beast" in Julius's mind wasn't just pacing now; it was clawing at the bars. The combination of the alcohol, the trauma of the last week, and Cynthia's suffocating proximity was a chemical reaction he couldn't stop. He felt his breathing hitch, his pulse thrumming in his ears like a war drum.

"You sign a contract to serve," she said, her hand moving to the back of his neck, her thumb grazing the sensitive skin behind his ear. "But you haven't even begun to understand what service means. It's not just about showing up, Julius. It's about surrender."

Julius looked down at her—at the powerful director who held his freedom in her clutch bag—and felt a wave of dizzying, dark attraction. He knew he shouldn't. He knew this was the trap, the gilded cage closing tight. But as she leaned in, her breath warm against his lips, the discipline he'd fought so hard to maintain over his hypersexual urges snapped like dry kindling.

"I told you," She breathed, her eyes locking onto his. "I only bite if you want me to."

Julius didn't answer with words. He reached out, his hands trembling as he gripped her waist, pulling her flush against him. The velvet and silk of the room blurred into the background as he leaned down, surrendering to the very thing he had promised himself he would conquer.

The contract was signed, the debt was paid, and as the lights of Detroit flickered outside the window, Julius Sterling realized he wasn't just replacing Daniel Vance's job—he was disappearing into his skin.

8

The atmosphere in the suite had shifted, the air thick and heavy with the scent of aged bourbon and the dangerous, electric tension that had been building since they left the bar. Cynthia stood in the center of the room, her silhouette framed by the glittering Detroit skyline.

"Take off your shirt," she commanded.

Her voice wasn't a request; it was a low, melodic vibration that brooked no argument. Julius found himself obeying instantly, the fabric of his dark Henley clearing his head to reveal the bruised, tense lines of his torso. He stood before her, feeling the cool air of the room hit his skin, but his blood was anything but cold. He was mesmerized by her dominant tone; there was a terrifying, addictive thrill in the way she spoke—as if he were already an extension of her will, a piece of property she was finally inspecting.

The "beast" he had tried so hard to cage since his youth roared to life. The hypersexual urges he usually fought with iron discipline were now fueled by the alcohol and the sheer power radiating from the woman before him. He felt the blood rush south, his pulse thrumming with a demanding heat as a visible, heavy bulge strained against the fabric of his boxers. He was fully, painfully erect, his body betraying every attempt at stoicism.

Cynthia didn't look away. Instead, she slowed her pace, a knowing, triumphant smile spreading across her lips.

Her eyes dropped to the unmistakable silhouette beneath his waistband, tracking the way he had reached his limit. She didn't seem shocked; she looked like a hunter who had finally cornered a prize she had already paid for.

Julius's breath hitched, coming in ragged, shallow bursts. As she stepped closer, the daring slit of her black dress fanned open, and his mind raced with the intoxicating, visceral realization that she was bare beneath the silk. He imagined her naked, her heat open to the very air he was struggling to breathe, the scent of her skin mingling with the expensive lavender of the room.

"You're a very reactive man, Julius," she whispered, stepping into the narrow space between his knees.

The silence of the suite was absolute, save for the sound of his own thudding heart. He looked into her eyes, his head light and his resolve crumbling into ash. He was no longer the man who had walked into the museum trying to find "therapy" in history. He was a man drowning in the present, and Cynthia Townsend was the only thing keeping him—or pulling him—under.

She took one more step, closing the distance until the heat from her body was a physical force against his bare chest. Julius stood rooted to the spot, his hands hovering at his sides, unsure if he was allowed to touch her or if he was simply meant to stand there and be consumed.

"I can feel your heart," she whispered, her eyes locked onto his with a frightening intensity. "It's trying to beat its way right out of your chest."

She didn't use her hands. Instead, she leaned in until her lips brushed against the shell of his ear, her breath a warm, humid caress. "Do you remember the contract, Julius? The part about loyalty? The part about *availability*?"

He let out a low, shaky breath, his eyes fluttering shut. The "beast" was no longer pacing; it was in control, a primal hunger that made his muscles ache. "I remember," he managed to choke out.

"Good." She pulled back as her smile grew sharper, more predatory. "Because tonight, I'm the only principal that matters. You aren't a specialist anymore. You aren't a defendant. You're exactly what I bought you to be."

Her hand finally moved, her fingers trailing slowly down his sternum, over his stomach, until they hooked into the waistband of his boxers. The contact was electric. Julius groaned, a sound of pure, helpless surrender that echoed in the quiet luxury of the suite. The scent of her—that dark, intoxicating mix of vanilla and power—was everywhere now, filling his lungs until he couldn't remember what it felt like to breathe on his own.

He reached out, his fingers finally finding the silk of her dress at the small of her back. He pulled her flush against him, feeling the devastating softness of her body against the rigid tension of his own. The city outside was a million lights and a million people, but for Julius, the world had shrunk down to the four walls of the Wellington and the woman who held his life in the palm of her hand.

His lips finally crashed against hers in a desperate, bruising kiss that tasted of bourbon and ruin. In that moment, the guilt of the accident and the fear of the cage vanished, replaced by a dark, gilded reality where his body was no longer his own, and the only escape was to go deeper into the fire.

She didn't stop at the waistband. Her fingers trailed lower, tracing the heavy, pulsing length of him through the thin cotton of his boxers. The contact was like a live wire hitting water; Julius gasped, his head snapping back as his eyes rolled into the back of his head. Every ounce of the discipline he'd spent years building—the therapy, the mantras, the cold showers—disintegrated in a single, agonizingly perfect second.

"Look at me," she whispered, her voice a sharp blade of command.

Julius forced his eyes open, his vision swimming. Cynthia stood so close that the heat of her naked skin, hidden just behind that thin layer of silk, radiated against his thighs. She reached for the side of her dress, her fingers finding the hem of the daring slit. With a slow, deliberate motion, she hiked the fabric up, exposing the smooth, unbroken line of her hip and the dark, shadowed curve of her groin.

He was right. There was nothing between her and the air.

The scent of her—rich, musky, and raw—hit him with the force of a tidal wave. It was an intoxicating, primal aroma that flooded his senses, drowning out the expensive lavender of the room. Julius felt a low, guttural growl vibrate in his chest.

The "beast" wasn't just awake; it was starving, and the feast was right in front of him.

"You've been holding back so much, haven't you?" Cynthia murmured, her eyes dark with a mix of lust and cruel triumph. She took his hand—the one that had signed the contract only hours before—and guided it toward the heat.

The moment his fingers brushed against her damp, velvet warmth, the world outside the Wellington ceased to exist. There was no manslaughter charge. There was no Maya. There was only the slick, sliding friction and the overwhelming realization that he had been purchased for exactly this.

Julius let out a ragged moan, his knees nearly buckling as he surged forward, his mouth finding the crook of her neck. He inhaled the scent of her skin, desperate and half-mad, while his fingers sank into her softness. He was no longer a man; he was a reaction, a creature of pure, unadulterated appetite.

Cynthia threw her head back, a sharp, triumphant breath escaping her as she gripped his hair, pulling him deeper into her. "That's it," she hissed. "Show me what I paid for, Julius."

The lights of Detroit continued to flicker through the window, but in the shadows of the suite, the last of Julius Sterling's old life was being burned away in a fever of silk, skin, and absolute surrender.

Julius didn't need another word of encouragement. The "beast" had broken its chains, fueled by the intoxicating scent of her nakedness and the crushing weight of the life he was leaving behind. He lifted her effortlessly, her legs wrapping around his waist as the silk of her dress bunched between them. He carried her the few steps to the bed, the motion fluid and desperate, until they collapsed into the deep, velvet blankets.

The Wellington suite was a blur of motion and stifling heat, the air thick with the scent of lavender and the heavy, musky musk of surrender. Julius was a man possessed, his movements driven by a hypersexual hunger that had been suppressed for far too long under the crushing weight of his recovery. He tasted the salt on her skin and the lingering bourbon on her breath, his hands exploring every inch of the woman who now owned him. Every time he felt the friction of her silk dress against his bare chest, the electric hum in his blood spiked, pushing him closer to a total loss of self.

Cynthia was a revelation in the dark—vocal, demanding, and entirely unafraid of the fire she had stoked. She arched beneath him on the expansive bed, her fingers digging into the muscles of his back, leaving jagged red marks that he couldn't even feel through the haze of adrenaline.

"Don't stop," she breathed against his ear, her voice a ragged ghost of its executive composure. "Don't you dare stop."

As the encounter reached a fever pitch, Julius felt a strange, terrifying sense of clarity. This was the "opportunity of a lifetime" she had promised. It wasn't just the money or the erased criminal record; it was the absolute, total permission to be the version of himself he feared most. In the heat of the moment, the shame felt like power, and the service felt like freedom.

The world narrowed down to the rhythm of their breathing and the slick, sliding heat of their bodies. When the first peak came, it was explosive—a shattering release that left Julius gasping for air, his forehead resting against the crook of her neck as his heart tried to hammer its way through his ribs.

"Suck it," he commanded, his voice a low, gravelly rasp.

Immediately, her glistening lips engulfed him. She took him in deeply; her eyes locked onto his with a predatory intensity. She worked her fingers over the shaft, licking and nibbling with a practiced skill that made him squirm in ecstasy. Julius reached over her, pulling at the silk of her top to free a breast. He pinched her nipple, making her moan around him as she continued her work. He felt the pressure mounting again, his body responding to the pace she set, and without warning, he erupted once more. He held her head there, forcing her to clean every bit of the evidence of his release.

When he finally released her, she looked up with a sexy, triumphant smile, licking her chin to catch the last of him. "Wow," she whispered, her voice husky. "You do have a lot in those young balls, don't you? How about you put that massive dick in my pussy, Julius? I want to feel you inside of me again."

She looked at him with pure lust, and Julius responded with a primal energy. He pulled her deeper into the center of the plush mattress, the silk sheets bunching beneath them.

"Fuck me, Julius," she screamed, her legs hooking around his waist. Make me your bitch! And fuck me now!"

He was already rock-hard again, fueled by the dirty talk and the intoxicating power dynamic. He pulled up her skirt, revealing exactly what he had hoped for: she wasn't wearing panties.

"Oh, you're a naughty girl," he told her, staring at the bare, damp heat of her. "Good girls wear panties."

"Good thing I'm not a good girl, then," she teased, her eyes flashing.

He leaned down and kissed her aggressively, their tongues tangling as he began to work his way down her body. He moved from her neck to her chest, tweaking and sucking her nipples until she was sobbing with pleasure. He moved further down, kissing her inner thighs and teasing her with the same agonizing patience she had shown him.

"OH, FUCK ME JULIUS!" she begged.

He finally pressed his face into her, smelling that deep, musky scent for the first time. It was a visceral, intoxicating aroma that turned him on more than the alcohol ever could. He pushed his tongue deep within her, and almost immediately, the sensation pushed her over the edge.

"FUUUUCK YES! OH, SHIT!" she shouted in ecstasy, her body writhing and her nails clawing at his back as she came hard in his mouth.

Exhausted, she relaxed for a moment, letting him clean her as she giggled breathlessly. "Shit," she said, her voice trembling. "That's the hardest I've come in years. You really know how to please a girl."

"Oh, I'm not done yet, Cynthia," he told her. "

He aimed his raging cock at her and slid in. She was incredibly wet, her body taking all seven inches of him in one hungry gulp. He started to fuck her, slowly at first, his eyes locked on her contorted face.

"Shit. Fuck. Shit," she cried with every thrust as he increased the pace. He rubbed her clit and sucked her nipples, the sound of their bodies colliding becoming a rhythmic, sloppy mess. He rammed in and out of her, her juices dripping onto the sheets as she shouted expletives into the quiet room.

"SHIT! FUCK! FUUUUUCK!" she screamed as she hit her second climax. He felt her pussy tightening like a vice around him, and he knew he was finished.

"Shit... I'm gunna cccooommmeee!" he cried, pulling out and shooting load after load onto her trim as their faces contorted together in the final, agonizing thrall of pleasure.

They lay there for a few minutes in the heavy silence that followed, exhausted and tangled in the wreckage of the bed. Silence eventually reclaimed the suite, broken only by the distant sound of a siren on the street below. Julius lay there, smelling the scent of her and the night, feeling the heavy, leaden weight of exhaustion settling into his bones. The adrenaline was fading, leaving behind the cold, hard reality of the pact he had sealed with his body.

Cynthia lay beside him, her chest rising and falling in steady intervals. She looked toward the window, where the first faint hint of grey was beginning to bleed into the Detroit sky. The dominant, predatory light was still in her eyes, but it was tempered now by a quiet, smug satisfaction. She had her investment, and she knew exactly how to use it.

The harsh, unforgiving light of a Detroit morning bled through the heavy velvet curtains of the Wellington, casting long, dusty streaks across the rumpled silk sheets. Julius stirred, the movement sending a sharp, stabbing reminder through his bruised ribs. The scent of the night—musk, expensive perfume, and sweat—still hung heavy in the stagnant air of the suite.

He sat up, his head throbbing with a dull bourbon ache, and watched Cynthia. She was already up, standing before a floor-to-ceiling mirror, sliding into her black dress with a clinical efficiency that made the previous night feel like a fever dream. She looked impeccable, her broad meeting mask firmly back in place as if she hadn't been screaming expletives into his ear just hours before.

"Dominic would like to see you," she said, her voice crisp and devoid of the night's husky warmth. She didn't look at him, focused instead on clasping a gold earring. "So, washed up and get dressed. We don't keep him waiting."

Julius felt a cold knot tighten in his stomach. The "partner." The man who shared her roof and her secrets. "Now?" he asked, his voice sounding raw and foreign to his own ears.

"Now," she affirmed, finally glancing at him through the mirror. Her gaze was cool, appraising, like a collector checking the condition of a new acquisition.

Julius stood and walked into the marble-clad bathroom. He splashed ice-cold water on his face, trying to shock the fog out of his brain. When he looked up, he was forced to face the man in the mirror. His eyes were bloodshot, and his back was a map of angry red scratches from Cynthia's nails—physical proof of the line he had crossed. He looked like a stranger. The man who had been trying to heal, the man who cared about "therapy" at the museum, was gone. In his place was the $180,000 investment.

He dressed quickly, his movements mechanical. Before he stepped out to meet the shark waiting in the living area, he pulled his phone from his pocket. He needed a tether to his real life before it drifted away entirely.

He dialed Jazmine. She picked up on the second ring, her voice thick with relief. "Julius? My god, are you okay? I was up all night."

"I'm alright, Jazz," he said, his voice softening, though the lie tasted like ash. "I'm sorry. Things got... complicated with the new firm."

"Where are you?"

"Still downtown. Look, I'm going to be working overnight for a while, handling a big account. I'll swing by the house later today to see you and Leo before I head back in." He gripped the phone tighter, staring at his reflection. "I'm okay, Jazmine. Really. This is just the opportunity I needed."

"Okay," she whispered, sounding unconvinced but desperate to believe him. "Just be safe. I love you, Julius."

"Love you too."

He hung up and took a steadying breath. He shoved the phone into his pocket, effectively burying the man who stayed at his sister's duplex. He stepped out of the bathroom into the suite, where Cynthia was waiting by the door, her hand on her hip.

"Ready?" she asked.

"Ready," Julius replied, his face a mask of iron.

9

The morning had dissolved into a sterile, professional silence. A black sedan, driven by a man whose expression was as tinted and impenetrable as the windows, was waiting at the curb of the Wellington. Julius sat in the back beside Cynthia, his ribs throbbing in rhythm with the car's tires hitting the uneven Detroit pavement.

As they moved north, the jagged skyline of downtown gave way to the lush, quiet dignity of the Palmer Woods neighborhood. The city's noise seemed to be filtered out by the canopy of ancient oaks and maples that arched over the winding roads. Here, the world felt insulated, preserved in a time of old-world ambition and heavy stone.

The car slowed as it turned onto a street where the houses looked less like dwellings and more like fortresses of heritage. The driver pulled into a semicircular driveway fronting a massive Timeless Tudor. It was a grand, sprawling residence, its dark brickwork and half-timbering standing in sharp contrast to the bright midday sun.

Julius stepped out of the car, his shoes crunching on the gravel. He looked up at the leaded-glass windows and the steep gables. The house had exceptional bones, a masterpiece of craftsmanship that felt like it was watching him.

"Stay close," Cynthia said, her voice a cool command as she smoothed her dress. "And let me do the talking. Dominic appreciates silence until he asks for a sound."

They walked toward the heavy oak door. The air here was different—cooler, smelling of damp earth and blooming hydrangeas. As they stepped inside, a welcoming foyer opened up, leading into a spacious living room where the sunlight fought its way through original plasterwork and rich millwork. To the left, a large wood-paneled library glowed with the amber hue of polished mahogany. It was exactly lunchtime. The house felt cavernous, filled with the scent of beeswax and expensive tobacco.

"Dominic?" Cynthia's voice echoed through the high ceilings.

"In the porch," a deep, resonant voice replied, coming from the back of the house.

She led Julius through the house, passing a generous screened porch designed for indoor-outdoor living. The architecture was a rare opportunity of restoration and preserved history, featuring terrazzo floors and four grand fireplaces that added an imposing warmth to the halls.

They found him sitting at a small table near a wall of leaded glass. Dominic was a man who looked like he had been carved out of the same dark wood as the library. He didn't look up from his meal immediately; instead, he carefully sliced a piece of steak, his movements precise.

"You're late, Cynthia," Dominic said, his tone neutral but heavy with an underlying edge.

"Traffic, Dominic," she replied easily, sliding into the chair opposite him. She gestured toward Julius, who stood near the entrance of the room, feeling the weight of the "investment" on his shoulders. "This is him. Julius Sterling."

Dominic finally looked up. His eyes were sharp, dissecting Julius with the clinical detachment of a man checking the teeth of a horse. "The man who signed the pact," he murmured. He set his fork down with a quiet *clink* against the China. "Come closer, Mr. Sterling. I want to see if the money we spent was worth the trouble you've caused."

Julius stepped forward into the light of the porch, the bruises on his face and the scratches on his back hidden beneath his clothes, but his soul felt entirely exposed.

The screened porch was an oasis of filtered light and quiet tension. Outside, the manicured gardens of Palmer Woods swayed in a light breeze, but inside, the air was still, heavy with the scent of seared steak and the faint, bitter aroma of the espresso Dominic was already sipping. The rich millwork of the house extended even here, with dark beams overhead and vintage tiles underfoot that spoke of a Detroit era built on steel and untouchable wealth.

Dominic didn't offer Julius a seat. He simply gestured with a silver knife toward the end of the table. A third plate had been set, though Julius felt less like a guest and more like a specimen under a microscope.

"Sit, Mr. Sterling," Dominic said, his voice a low, gravelly baritone. "The help prepared a blackened ribeye. *Eat.* You look like a man who has spent the last twenty-four hours exhausting himself."

The comment was pointed, a sharp needle hidden in a velvet glove. Cynthia didn't flinch; she picked up her wine glass, the liquid catching the midday sun. Julius sat, the leather of the chair creaking under his weight. His appetite was nonexistent, his stomach still a tight knot of bourbon and nerves, but he picked up his fork.

"Cynthia tells me you have a certain... presence," Dominic continued, leaning back. "That you handled the situation at the museum with a level of stoicism that Daniel lacked. Daniel was a frantic creature. He didn't understand that in this house, we value the silence between the words more than the words themselves."

"I'm just here to do the job," Julius said, his voice steady despite the thrumming of his heart.

Dominic chuckled, a dry, humorless sound. "The job. He thinks it's a job, Cynthia. How charming." He turned his sharp, predatory gaze back to Julius. "You aren't a clock-puncher anymore. You are a ghost. You drive when we say drive, you stand where we say stand, and you provide... comfort... when the principals require it. In exchange, your 'accident' with the pedestrian becomes a footnote in a file that will never see the light of a courtroom."

Julius felt the weight of the Tudor house pressing down on him. The leaded-glass windows seemed to distort the outside world, making the trees and the street look like a distant, unreachable dream. "I understand the stakes," Julius replied, meeting Dominic's gaze.

"Do you?" Dominic leaned forward, the shadows of the porch eaves falling across his face. "Because the moment you stepped into the Wellington last night, you stopped belonging to the city of Detroit, nor your family. You belong to the pact, your new family. If you fail us—or if you fail her—there isn't a hole deep enough in this state to hide you from the consequences."

Cynthia reached out, her fingers grazing the base of her glass. "He won't fail, Dominic. I've already seen his potential. He has a hunger that matches our own."

"Cynthia tells me you're a man who knows how to keep a secret," Dominic said, his voice a low rumble. "But I don't care about what you keep in your pockets, son. "I want to know what you keep in your gut. There's a tension in your jaw—a 'beast' that's trying to chew its way out. Where did a boy like you get a shadow that long?"

Julius looked at the sprawling, perfectly manicured lawn, feeling the familiar prickle of heat at the back of his neck.

The honesty came out not because he wanted to share, but because Dominic's presence demanded it.

Juluis repeats his story from the night before. Dominic didn't flinch. He didn't offer a look of pity, which was the first thing that made Julius trust him.

"Mentally, it turned my head into a hall of mirrors. Physically, I grew up too fast, and socially, I became a ghost. I learned how to be whatever a she wanted me to be just to survive the hour. I've spent my life trying to outrun the shame of it, but the 'beast' you, see? That's just the armor I grew over the wounds."

Dominic let out a long, slow breath, the smoke from his nearby cigar curling into the air. He leaned forward, the wood of his chair creaking.

"We all have our origins, Julius," Dominic said, his voice surprisingly gentle. "Mine was the street; yours was a bedroom. But the result is the same. You've been shaped by a fire that would have melted most men. You've lived your life as a victim of that beast, letting it drive you into rooms you didn't want to be in. I'm offering you a chance to put a leash on it."

Dominic reached out, tapping a heavy finger on the arm of his chair. "In this world, that trauma isn't a weakness. It's the ultimate preparation. You know how to read people because you had to read *her* to stay safe. You know how to please because you had to please *her* to keep the peace. Now, you're going to do it for us. And in return, the beast gets fed, and your family stays in the sun."

Julius looked up at the man who would become his mentor, his savior, and eventually, his ghost. In that moment, the bargain was struck. He wasn't being hired; he was being claimed. Dominic looked between them, a slow, knowing smirk spreading across his face. He reached for a linen napkin and wiped his mouth with meticulous care. "I see. You've already broken him in. Efficient as always, Cynthia."

He turned back to Julius, his eyes narrowing. "Eat your lunch, Mr. Sterling. After this, you're going back to your sister's. Pack a bag. You'll be staying at the Wellington tonight. Mrs. Alistair has heard quite a bit about your... stamina. She's looking forward to seeing if the rumors are true."

The steak tasted like iron in Julius's mouth. He looked at the four fireplaces visible through the open doors of the interior rooms, symbols of warmth and home that now felt like the mouths of furnaces. He was being fed, housed, and clothed by monsters, and as he caught Cynthia's icy, triumphant wink from across the table, he realized the lunch wasn't a welcome—it was a final inspection. Julius set his fork down, the silver clattering against the China with a sharp, dissonant ring. He looked from Cynthia to Dominic, the reality of his situation settling in like a heavy fog.

"The files," Julius began, his voice low and cautious. "The evidence of the crash. How exactly do you eliminate something like that? The police have photos, witnesses, a body. You can't just make it disappear."

Dominic leaned back, a slow, predatory smile spreading across his face. He exchanged a brief, knowing look with Cynthia before turning his gaze back to Julius.

"Eliminate them?" Dominic echoed, as if the idea were quaint. "Mr. Sterling, we don't destroy information. Information is a resource. We simply... recontextualize it."

Cynthia took a sip of her wine, her eyes watching Julius over the rim of the glass. "If we simply deleted the files, it would leave a vacuum. Vacuums invite questions from nosy detectives and insurance adjusters. We don't want questions."

"Then what?" Julius asked, his brow furrowed.

"The responsibility for the crash will be placed on someone else," Dominic explained, his tone as casual as if he were discussing the weather. "Specifically, someone who doesn't exist. You're a casualty of the accident. Our associates have already crafted a digital footprint for a man—a temporary worker from overseas. We have the logs, the simulated witness statements, and a 'confession' signed in a language most of the precinct won't bother to translate."

Julius felt a chill run down his spine. "And the family? The people who lost someone?"

"The family will be given closure," Cynthia said, her voice dropping into the rehearsed, empathetic tone she used for the cameras. "They will be told that the suspect was apprehended late last night. To avoid a lengthy and painful trial, he pleaded guilty. In exchange for his immediate deportation and the permanent revocation of his visa, the state agreed not to pursue a prison sentence. He is already 'on a plane' back to a village that doesn't have a paved road, let alone an extradition treaty. He will never return to the United States."

Julius stared at them, horrified by the clinical precision of the lie. A man's life had been ended, and they were replacing the truth with a phantom—a ghost that would take Julius's sins across the ocean and vanish.

"So, the case is closed," Julius whispered. "Just like that."

"Wrapped in a bow," Dominic said, picking up his espresso cup. "The police get a win, the family gets their 'justice,' and the city moves on. Everyone is satisfied, provided you remain... useful."

The grand Tudor house, with its rich millwork and timeless architecture, suddenly felt like a tomb. Julius realized that the "freedom" they had given him was built on a foundation of absolute deception. He wasn't just a driver or a consultant; he was a secret that required an entire alternate reality to keep hidden.

"Now," Dominic said, the espresso cup clicking against the saucer. "Finish your meal. You have a long night ahead of you at the Wellington, and I expect you to be at your best for Mrs. Alistair."

The shadows on the screened porch deepened as a cloud passed over the Palmer Woods sun, turning the lush greenery outside into silhouettes against the leaded glass. Dominic set his linen napkin aside, his eyes never leaving Julius's face.

"Cynthia, darling," Dominic said, his voice smooth but layered with an unmistakable iron authority. "Would you mind giving us the room? I'd like a private moment with our new associate to discuss the finer points of his itinerary."

Cynthia didn't hesitate. She stood with a graceful rustle of silk, her expression unreadable. She leaned down, pressing a lingering, possessive kiss to Dominic's cheek before turning that same sharp, triumphant gaze toward Julius. "Don't be too hard on him, Dom. I've only just gotten him broken in."

With a soft click of her heels against the terrazzo floor, she vanished into the depths of the Tudor mansion, leaving a vacuum of silence behind her. Dominic waited until the sound of her footsteps faded completely. He reached into a humidor on the table, clipped a dark cigar with surgical precision, and lit it. The thick, blue smoke curled toward the rich wood beams of the ceiling.

"You've met my daughter, Carla," Dominic began, his eyes narrowing through the haze. "The woman at the museum who courted your friend away from you. The one who manages the... logistical side of our principals' needs."

Julius nodded, his throat dry. "I remember her."

"Good. Because from this moment forward, Carla is your shadow. But more importantly, she is your gatekeeper." Dominic leaned forward, the smell of expensive tobacco and old power washing over Julius. "Your first order is simple, yet absolute: You tell Carla everything. Every whim Mrs. Alistair expresses tonight, every twitch of her hand, every glass of water she drinks. If she asks you to drive her to the moon, you tell Carla before you put the car in gear."

Julius felt the cage tightening. "She's, my handler."

"She is your lifeline," Dominic corrected sharply, tapping ash into a crystal tray. "Mrs. Alistair is... a woman of delicate and often volatile appetites. She is one of the most powerful donors in this city, and her discretion is as fragile as thin ice. If she tries to lead you off the path—if she tries to involve you in anything outside the scope of the pact—you report it to Carla immediately. You do not think. You do not hesitate. You do not try to be a hero."

Dominic stood up, his tall frame blocking out the afternoon light. He walked around the table until he was standing directly over Julius, his presence as heavy as the stone walls of the house.

"Carla will meet you at the Wellington tonight at 8:00 PM. She will have the key, the itinerary, and the specific... requirements for the evening. You will treat her word as if it came from my own mouth. If Carla says jump, you don't ask how high; you simply leave the ground."

He reached out, gripping Julius's shoulder with a hand that felt like a meat hook. "Tonight isn't about pleasure, Sterling. It's about performance. You are the product we sold. If Mrs. Alistair isn't satisfied, that phantom we created to take the fall for the crash? He might just find a reason to come back to the country and name his real accomplice."

The threat hung in the air, cold and undeniable. The beautiful Tudor architecture, the vintage tiles, and the smell of lunch suddenly felt like a decorated slaughterhouse.

"I understand," Julius whispered, the weight of the scratches on his back and the contract in his soul feeling heavier than ever.

"See that you do," Dominic said, releasing him. "Now get out of my house. Go see your family. Remind yourself what you're fighting to keep, because by tomorrow morning, you'll be a different man entirely."

Julius stood, his legs feeling heavy, like he was wading through deep water. He walked away from the light of the porch, moving back through the grand, silent house. He passed the wood-paneled library and the sprawling living room, the weight of the Tudor's history pressing in on him. He felt like a ghost haunting a museum of a life he would never truly own.

Behind him, in the solitude of the porch, the silence was suddenly shattered. A wet, ragged sound tore through the air—a cough so violent it seemed to vibrate against the leaded-glass windows. Julius stopped in the foyer, his hand on the heavy oak door handle. He looked back, but he stayed out of sight, caught in a moment of morbid hesitation.

Dominic had doubled over, his powerful frame suddenly looking fragile against the backdrop of his vast estate. He fumbled for the linen napkin on the table, pressing it hard against his mouth. The coughing fit lasted for several agonizing seconds, a deep, rattling labor that sounded like something tearing deep inside his chest.

When the fit finally subsided, Dominic pulled the handkerchief away. Julius, squinting through the doorway, saw the splash of vivid, arterial crimson against the pristine white fabric. It wasn't just a speck; it was a heavy, dark stain that spoke of a clock ticking toward midnight.

Dominic stared at the blood for a long, quiet beat. There was no fear in his expression—only a bitter, weary annoyance. He folded the napkin with meticulous care, hiding the stain deep within the fabric, and shoved it into the pocket of his tailored trousers. He stood up, straightened his vest, and took a slow, steadying breath. He cleared his throat, adjusted his cuffs, and reached for his espresso cup as if nothing had happened.

The secret stayed trapped within those stone walls, a terminal truth buried beneath a mask of absolute control. Dominic was a man building a legacy on secrets, even as his own body began to betray him. Julius stepped out of the heavy shadows of the foyer, his mind still reeling from the weight of Dominic's threats. Before he could reach the front door, Cynthia emerged from the amber light of the library. She wasn't empty-handed.

She held a high-quality leather duffel bag, which she set down on a vintage bench with a heavy *thud.* Her expression was no longer the hungry, predatory one from the Wellington; it was the cold, efficient face of a woman who managed assets.

"A few essentials for your transition," she said, her voice echoing off the original plasterwork of the hall. She unzipped the bag just enough for him to see the contents: a thick envelope stuffed with cash, a flip phone, and a set of forged identification documents. "If the world falls apart—if the pact is breached and you need to vanish—that is your head start. Don't use it unless the sky is falling."

She reached into her pocket and handed him a sleek, brand-new smartphone. "Your new lifeline. My number and Carla's are already programmed. Toss that piece of shit of your old phone in the trash." She then slid a small embossed card toward him. "This is an address in Birmingham. Go there before you see your sister. They have three suits and three casual sets waiting for you. High-thread count and they will tailor the suits for your frame. You represent us now; you will no longer be dressing like a man who works for a common most of the time. Whatever you wear on your "off time" is up to you."

Finally, she handed him a small leather card holder. Inside was a work card along with an insurance and registration card. Julius frowned, flipping the insurance and registration over.

"What arc these for? I don't have a car."

Cynthia offered a small, enigmatic smile—one that didn't reach her eyes.

"You do now."

She led him out onto the gravel driveway. The afternoon sun was blinding after the dim interior of the Tudor. Parked directly behind the sedan that had brought them was a brand-new Lexus LS. Its black paint was so deep and polished it looked like a pool of ink, reflecting the ancient trees of Palmer Woods. The chrome accents glinted, and the windows were tinted to a legal limit that still felt like a shroud.

"The insurance and registration are for this," she said, gesturing to the vehicle. "It's armored to a Level 4 standard. It's quiet, it's fast, and it's yours to maintain. It is the only place outside of this house where you are truly safe."

Julius walked toward the machine, his hand hovering over the cold metal. He felt the gravity of it—the Lexus wasn't just a car; it was a mobile office, a gilded cage on wheels that signaled his permanent entry into their world.

"The tank is full," Cynthia added, watching him with an unreadable gaze. "Go to Birmingham then Dearborn. Say your goodbyes to the life you knew, Julius. By tonight, the man who lived in that duplex will be a ghost."

Julius took the keys from her hand, the weight of the fob heavy in his palm. He climbed into the driver's seat, the scent of fresh leather and high-end electronics filling his lungs. As he pulled out of the winding, tree-lined streets of Palmer Woods, the Lexus moved with a ghostly silence, isolating him from the very city he had grown up in.

Julius arrived at the Dearborn duplex around 4:30 pm. The neighborhood looked gray and tired against the shimmering back paint of the Lexus LS. He slipped inside quietly; the silent engine having left no warning of his arrival. Jazmine was in the kitchen, the low hum of the radio masking his movements.

As he moved toward the back of the house, his heart hammered against his ribs. It was then he saw the mail of the dining table. The orange eviction notice was a punch to the gut-two months late. While Jazmine's back was turned, he snatched the envelope and tucked it into his pocket, the paper crinkling against his hip.

"Julius?' she called out, turning with a glass water, her eyes red-rimmed from lack of sleep.

He didn't give her the chance to see the panic in his eyes. The weight of the notice in his pocket made the air in the small house feel thin.

"I have to go, Jazz," he interrupted, his voice clipped. "I've got to run some errands before I head back to work. It's going to be a long night."

"But you just got here," she protested, her voice breaking.

"I'll see you tomorrow, and we can talk about everything, I promise."

He turned away before she could see the lie written on his face. He stepped back out to the Lexus, the silent machine waiting to carry him away from the decay of his old life. The drive to Birmingham felt like a journey into a different country. The Lexus glided through the upscale streets, its interior a sanctuary from the rattling transit buses and sirens he had just left behind. Julius found the address Cynthia had given him-a discreet, high-end boutique with no sign on the door, only a gold-leafed crest.

Inside, the air was chilled and smelled of cedar and expensive wool. A man in a charcoal waistcoat greeted Julius without a word, leading him to a private dressing room where three bespoke suits and three sets of casual attire-cashmere sweaters and slacks-were already laid out like armor.

Julius changed into the suit he will wearing for tonight. The fabric felt like a second skin, erasing the rough-up, desperate man who had just stood in a crumbling Dearborn kitchen. He draped two of the suits into high-quality garment bags and headed back to the car, layering the expensive clothes over the stacks of cash and the forged documents.

As he pulled away from the curb, the weight of the eviction notices in his pocket felt lighter, eclipsed by the sheer power of the machine he commanded and the "blood money" stashed in the truck. He wasn't the man from the duplex anymore.

10

The sun was beginning to dip below the jagged Detroit horizon, casting long, bruised shadows across the pavement as Julius pulled the Lexus LS into the valet circle of the Wellington Hotel. The building was a monolith of glass and steel, glowing with an artificial, golden warmth that promised a level of luxury most people only saw in movies.

Julius handed the keys to the valet, his movements stiff. The midnight-black suit he had kept in the car now felt like a second skin—perfectly tailored, sharp, and cold. In his pocket, the crumpled eviction notices from the duplex felt like a lead weight, reminding him exactly why he was standing in a lobby that smelled of expensive orchids and filtered air.

Carla was waiting for him near the elevators. She looked different than she had at the museum; her sleek, charcoal dress had been replaced by a sharp, professional suit that made her appear even more like a shadow come to life. Her eyes skipped over his face, noting the way the high-end concealer he'd applied earlier almost—but not quite—hid the fading bruises.

"You're five minutes early," she said, her voice a low, neutral vibration. "Dom appreciates punctuality. It suggests a man who understands that his time no longer belongs to him."

She swiped a gold-embossed keycard against the elevator's sensor. The doors slid open with a hushed whisper. As they ascended, the lights of the city began to spread out beneath them, a glittering carpet of broken dreams and hidden power.

"Listen closely," Carla said, not looking at him. "Mrs. Alistair is in the Presidential Suite. She is a woman of... specific requirements. She is a high-level donor with a reputation for being 'difficult.' Your job is to ensure that by the time the sun comes up, she considers herself the most satisfied woman in the state."

The elevator chimed, and the doors opened into a private foyer. Carla stopped and turned to face him, her expression a mask of clinical detachment.

"You report everything to me," she reminded him, her voice dropping an octave. "If she asks for something outside the protocol, you call me. If she becomes volatile, you call me. But above all, Julius, remember: you are the product. Do not let the brand suffer."

She handed him a small, translucent earpiece and a heavy brass keycard. "Room 4202. She's expecting you."

Julius took the key, his fingers grazing Carla's cold skin. He walked down the plushily carpeted hallway, the silence of the Wellington feeling more oppressive than the noise of the streets. He reached the double mahogany doors of the suite and paused. He thought of Jazmine's tired eyes, of Leo's plastic truck, and the bag of cash hidden under the old coats in the closet.

He placed the keycard to the sensor, unlocking the door. The suite was vast, lit only by the amber glow of the city through floor-to-ceiling windows. The air was thick with the scent of expensive gin and a sharp, floral perfume that felt like a warning.

"You're late," a voice called out from the shadows near the window.

Mrs. Alistair stepped into the light. She was older than Cynthia, with eyes that looked like they had seen everything and found most of it boring. She held a crystal glass in one hand, her gaze raking over Julius with a slow, predatory hunger that made his skin crawl.

"Well," she murmured, a slow smile spreading across her painted lips. "At least the investment looks like it has some stamina."

Mrs. Alistair didn't move from the window. She stood framed against the sprawling skyline, her silhouette sharp and imposing. She was still in her silk emerald-colored business entire that seemed to drink the moonlight, and as she turned fully toward him, the light caught the ice in her eyes. She wasn't just wealthy; she was a woman who carried her power like a weapon she was eager to test.

"Close the door, Julius," she commanded. It wasn't a request. "And don't just stand there like a statue. I didn't pay for a piece of furniture."

Julius obeyed, the heavy mahogany door clicking shut with a finality that made his heart thud against his ribs. He felt the earpiece Carla had given him resting cold against his skin, a silent witness to the night ahead.

"I'm here to ensure you have everything you need, Mrs. Alistair," Julius said, his voice dropping into the steady, professional tone he had practiced in the mirror.

She laughed, a sharp, brittle sound that echoed off the marble floors. She set her gin on a side table and walked toward him, her movements slow and deliberate. As she got closer, the scent of her perfume—Laverne and something metallic—filled his senses. She stopped just inches from him, her gaze traveling from his polished shoes up to the bruises she knew were hidden beneath his collar.

"Cynthia tells me you're quite a find," she whispered, reaching out a manicured hand to trace the line of his jaw. Her touch was cold, her nails sharp. "A man with a secret. Those are always the best kind. They have so much more to lose, which makes them so much more... compliant."

She stepped behind him, her silk jacket rustling like a snake in the grass. Julius felt her breath against the back of his neck, sending a chill down his spine that had nothing to do with desire.

"Tell me, Julius," she murmured, her voice vibrating right against his ear. "Are you prepared to be whatever I want you to be tonight? Because I find that 'newcomers' usually have a very limited range. I'm looking for someone who can handle the curves."

She moved back around to face him, her eyes dark with a mix of boredom and burgeoning cruelty. She reached out and gripped his tie, tugging him downward until their faces were level. "I want to see the beast Cynthia whispered about. I want to see if that $180,000 was a charity donation or an actual purchase."

Julius felt the familiar, dark heat rising in his chest—the "beast" Dominic had mentioned. It was the only part of him that felt real in this gilded nightmare. He looked into Mrs. Alistair's eyes, and for a moment, the roles shifted. He wasn't just an escort; he was a man with his back against a wall, and she was the only way out.

"I'll be whatever you need," Julius rasped, his hand finding the small of her back, pulling her flush against the midnight-black fabric of his suit. Mrs. Alistair's breath hitched, a flicker of genuine surprise crossing her face before it was replaced by a look of pure, unadulterated triumph. "Good," she hissed, her fingers digging into his shoulders. "Then start by showing me exactly how grateful you are to be out of that jail cell."

The emerald silk felt like cool water under Julius's palms, but the heat radiating from Mrs. Alistair was scorched and demanding. She didn't want the practiced romance of a lover; she wanted the raw, desperate energy of a man who had everything to lose.

Julius didn't hesitate. He swung her around, pressing her back against the floor-to-ceiling glass of the suite. The entire city of Detroit laid out behind her, a million flickering lights witnessing the transaction. He claimed her mouth with an aggression that bordered on a snarl, his hands tangling in her hair as she arched against him, her heels clicking rhythmically against the glass.

"That's it," she gasped against his lips, her voice ragged. "Forget the suit. Forget the manners. Show me the man who didn't care who he had to run over to survive."

The encounter was a fever of friction and sharp power plays. Mrs. Alistair was a woman used to being obeyed in galleries, and she brought that same cutting authority to the bedroom. To her, Julius wasn't a partner; he was a tool of release, a living monument to the debt he owed to the inner circle. She commanded his every move with the cold precision of a director, her nails leaving fresh tracks across his shoulders that marked him as hers, overriding the fading marks left by Cynthia the night before.

Julius moved with the predatory grace of a man who knew exactly what his silence was worth, but tonight, he was the physical manifestation of her demands. He swung her around with effortless strength, her back colliding with the floor-to-ceiling glass of the penthouse. Behind her, the sprawling skyline of Detroit was a silent, glittering witness. The glass was ice against her spine, a stark contrast to the radiating heat of the man she had summoned for her own gratification.

He claimed her mouth with a raw aggression that bordered on a snarl, but Mrs. Alistair met it with her own biting hunger. This wasn't the polished charm he wore for the city's matriarchs; this was the visceral reality she required to feel alive. His hands tangled deep into her hair, forcing her head back to expose her throat, while the rhythmic *click-click-click* of her designer heels against the glass sounded like a countdown.

When his tongue pushed past her teeth, she didn't just accept him—she took him. The power dynamic was a shimmering, unstable thing. She was the one with the influence, the one who decided if his "donations" were enough to keep him in the city's good graces, yet she allowed herself the thrill of his physical dominance. A wave of dark satisfaction washed over her. Against every moral fiber she possessed, she was enjoying the chaos of using him.

As abruptly as the storm had started, he tore his lips away, breathing hard. Mrs. Alistair stood there for a moment, chest heaving, her eyes burning with a sharp, regal intensity. She didn't sink to her knees out of weakness; she descended with the deliberate grace of a woman claiming what was hers. Julius looked down at her, a dark, transactional triumph gleaming in his eyes. He guided her fingers toward the heavy, unmistakable bulge straining against the fine silk of his slacks.

"Come on, Mrs. Alistair," he rasped, his voice dropping to a gravelly command. "Stroke it. Show me how much you want this."

He guided her fingers in a slow, torturous rhythm. She let out a sound that was less a whimper and more a soft, authoritative hum of approval.

"What's the matter?" Julius mocked, leaning closer until his scent—expensive cologne and raw heat—wrapped around her. "Shocked by what a real man looks like when he's not on a socialite's leash? Just imagine how it's going to feel when I'm buried deep inside you." The words were crude, stripping away the professional decorum she had cultivated for decades. As a donor, he should have been respectful; as an escort, he should have known his place. But Mrs. Alistair found the insolence arousing. It was the only thing sharp enough to cut through her stress.

Without a word, she reached for his belt buckle. Her movements were efficient, her fingers working the leather and expensive fabric with the same focus she used to close multi-million-dollar deals. She freed him from his confines, her breath hitching as he spilled into her hands. He was massive. Her analytical mind tried to calculate the scale of him—the sheer girth was staggering. She wondered idly how a man who lived his life in the shadows of powerful women managed to contain such a primal force.

Compelled by an authority she refused to relinquish, she reached out. Her right hand closed around his thick, veiny shaft while her left sought the warmth beneath. She realized with a jolt of heat that he was so thick her fingers couldn't even meet on the other side. Driven by a desperate curiosity—and the intent to master him—she leaned in. She trailed her lips over the broad, velvet-smooth head of his member, her tongue tasting him with a predatory hunger. In that moment, the "polished" Mrs. Alistair was gone, replaced by the woman who took exactly what she wanted from the men she owned.

The reality of the situation settled into her chest like a stone. Mrs. Alistair was horrified by the speed of her own submission, yet the logic that usually governed her life—the protocols of a high-stakes fundraiser, the decorum of Detroit's elite—had been suspended. In its place was a primal, feverish instinct. She felt Julius's heavy palms pressing down on the crown of her head, anchoring her as she ground her lips against the staggering width of his shaft. Her hands worked in a frantic, rhythmic harmony; one wrapped tightly around the pulsing length, the other kneading the heavy warmth beneath, pausing only to catch the salty beads of moisture from the crown.

"Fuck, you've got a sweet mouth, bitch" he groaned, his hips rocking in a slow, hypnotic friction.

Any other day, such a foul label would have earned him a stinging slap or a cold exit. But Julius was no ordinary man; he was a power consulting in a designer suit and an escort whose time was bought by the city's most formidable women. A perverse sense of pride surged through her. The knowledge that she—the refined, untouchable Mrs. Alistair—was pleasing a man of such dark reputation acted like an intoxicant. Her tongue flicked with renewed fervor, tracing the ridges of his rock-hard length.

Suddenly, the rhythm broke. Julius twisted his fingers into her hair, yanking her head back with a sharp tug that forced her eyes to meet his dark, blown-out pupils. He held her firm, his grip unyielding as he began to drive himself deeper. The mushroom-shaped head of his member pushed past her defenses, burying itself at the very back of her throat.

He was relentless. She felt the heat of him churning against her chin, the intrusion so deep it triggered a frantic, rhythmic gagging. Julius didn't care. He was a man possessed, his breath coming in ragged hitches as he prepared to break.

"Suck! Suck! Suck!" he chanted, the command vibrating through his entire frame.

Mrs. Alistair was forced to work her lips in a desperate, sliding motion along the velvet-tough skin. His moans grew louder, echoing off the glass walls of the penthouse. His fingers tightened their knot in her hair, pulling her face flush against his musty, masculine scent. With one final, almost brutal thrust, his body stiffened. She felt him extend, a final surge of dominance, and then he erupted.

The pulses were impossible to ignore. Each twitch of his anatomy sent a thick, hot jet down her throat. She gasped, unable to believe the sheer volume of his release. It flooded her mouth like heavy cream; what she couldn't swallow found its way into her breathing passages, leaving her face a dripping, undignified mess.

When he finally pulled away moments later, the silence of the room felt deafening. Her face was a ruin of his making. She knelt there on the plush carpet, the weight of her choices crashing down on her. She felt like a caricature of the woman she was supposed to be—less like a director of a foundation and more like a cheap hire in a dark alley. She couldn't comprehend how her life had derailed so spectacularly in the span of a single meeting.

Julius took a step back, and she lifted her head, her gaze trembling. To her utter shock, his erection remained as defiant and rigid as a flagpole in the wind, swaying slightly with his movement.

"Take off your jacket," he ordered, his voice cold and devoid of the previous heat.

Mrs. Alistair looked up at him, a fleeting spark of defiance flickering in her mind. For a second, she considered standing up and walking out into the night. But even as the thought formed, her muscles were already betraying her. She reached up, shrugging the expensive fabric from her shoulders and discarding it to the side.

He stepped back into her personal space, his eyes locked on hers. She waited, wondering if he would force her mouth to work again, but instead, he reached down. His hands, large and cruel, pressed firmly over the silk of her bared chest.

He began to fondle her breasts with a rough, territorial hunger, the touch of a man who knew he had bought every inch of her.

Mrs. Alistair closed her eyes, willing the man to stop, praying for her dignity to return. But as crude and vulgar as his touch was, she felt the traitorous peak of her nipples hardening against his palms, responding to the very menace she claimed to despise.

"Hmm. Not so prim and prissy now, are we, Mrs. Alistair?"

The mockingly formal use of her title felt like a slap, but she met his gaze with a cold, flickering intensity. She was used to being the one holding the gavel, the one whose signature decided the fate of city projects. Before she could process the shift in his tone, Julius used both hands to grip the lapels of her blouse, wrenching the fine silk apart with a violent tear. Buttons skittered across the floor like tiny, frantic insects, leaving her lace bra suddenly exposed to the cool air of the suite. He ran a proprietary hand over the curve of each breast, his touch less like a lover's and more like a high-end auditor assessing a new acquisition. He then ran his fingers back into her hair, and with a sharp, sudden tug, he swung her backward.

Mrs. Alistair hit the floor hard. The plush carpet did little to soften the shock to her system, but she didn't let out a cry; she merely exhaled, her eyes narrowing even as her heart hammered against her ribs. Julius took several deliberate steps until he was straddling her, a dark shadow blocking out the Detroit skyline. She watched, mesmerized by her own horror, as he slid a hand along his shaft and flicked the last remaining drop of his release onto her ruined blouse. He laughed—a dark, low sound that vibrated in the space between them.

"Spread your legs, Mrs. Alistair," he ordered, his voice echoing against the floor-to-ceiling glass. "Show me that unsatisfied pussy of yours."

The crudeness of the command sent a jolt of panic through her, yet even as her thoughts flashed to the daughter she was trying to protect and the professional reputation she had built, a different part of her—the part that thrived on the cutthroat nature of her work—responded to the raw demand for transparency. Mrs. Alistair obeyed, parting her thighs. She could feel the dampness of her own arousal straining against the thin lace of her panties, a visceral betrayal of her supposed disgust.

Julius stepped back slightly, his gaze traveling upward beneath the hem of her risen skirt. "Nice. I think I'm going to enjoy sticking my dick in your pussy, Mrs. Alistair."

"Then go ahead and do it! Get it over with!" she snapped. Her voice didn't waver; it carried the same sharp, cutting authority she used to end a stalled board meeting. She wanted the transaction finalized.

"Ah, well, you see, it's not as simple as all that," Julius countered, a predatory grin spreading across his face. "First, you have to tell me how much you want it."

"I don’t! You disgust me!" she countered, the authority in her voice warring with the visible tremble of her hands.

"Bullshit." He reached down, his palm flat against her bra-covered chest, his thumb tracing the frantic, erratic beat of her heart. "I saw how you sucked on me. I saw how you took my cum. You want it, bitch… and you want it bad. I just want to hear you say it."

She tried to form a denial, but her body had staged a mutiny. She realized then that he wouldn't be satisfied until she uttered the kind of filth she had spent her career excising from her world.

"Tell me your pussy is hot for my dick," he leered, leaning down until his breath hitched against her ear. "Tell me how good it’s going to feel in your married pussy."

"I can’t," she sobbed, the first tear finally breaking free, though her jaw remained set in a stubborn line of defiance.

Julius didn't offer comfort. He reached down and hooked a finger over the edge of her bra, pulling the cup away to expose her left breast. He gripped the raw, sensitive nipple, twisting it with a firm, painful pressure. "Say it!"

"Okay! Okay, I'll do it!" she shrieked, the sharp sting breaking her remaining resolve.

"Then start talking, or I'll pull this goddamn nipple right off your tit."

Mrs. Alistair squeezed her eyes shut, her dignity crumbling into the carpet. "Fuck me," she bleated, the words feeling like a signed confession. "Stick your big, hard cock in my pussy and... and fuck me."

"You want it bad, don't you, Mrs. Alistair?"

"Yes, I want it! Stick your prick in my pussy and cum just like you did in my mouth!"

Julius let out a triumphant laugh. "Sure, anytime you want."

He dropped to his knees between her legs. His hands worked their way up, pushing her skirt higher until her panties were fully exposed. With a sudden, violent motion, he grabbed the crotch of the fabric and ripped it clean away. Mrs. Alistair gasped, a final tear forming as she realized those were the panties her husband had recently bought for her. She held her breath, bracing for the inevitable intrusion, but Julius eased back, hovering just out of reach, prolonging the agony of her anticipation while the city of Detroit watched in silence.

Julius watched her from his height, his expression a mask of cold, predatory triumph. Looking down at the broken elegance of Mrs. Alistair, he felt a surge of power that far outweighed the physical thrum in his veins. He hadn't just taken her; he had unmade her. To a man who moved through the world as an escort for the elite, a high-priced shadow in the service of Detroit's most powerful women, this was the ultimate payout. He was no longer the one being directed or hired; he was the architect of her destruction.

As he watched her fingers disappear into herself, his internal monologue shifted from simple lust to a dark, calculative pride. He had seen women like her in boardrooms at his previous job—poised, untouchable, their spines a rod of iron. Now, that iron had melted under the heat of his gaze. Every time she uttered a word like *pussy* or *fuck*, he felt the thrill of a conqueror. He was stripping away the layers of the "concerned mother" and the "respectable professional" until there was nothing left but the raw, weeping nerves of a woman he had broken to his will.

"That's better," he murmured, his voice a low vibration that seemed to anchor her to the carpet.

He noticed the exact moment her performance died and the genuine ecstasy took over. It was in the way her pupils dilated, swallowing the iris whole, and the way her hips lost their hesitant jerkiness and began to roll with a primal, desperate hunger against the floor. He saw the "jar of honey" she had created coating her knuckles, and it stoked a fire in him that was less about affection and more about total ownership. He had reached inside her mind and rewired it, replacing the memory of her husband's face and her daughter's voice with the jagged rhythm of his own crude commands.

When she reached out and grabbed him, her fingers slick with the evidence of her own betrayal, Julius felt a jolt of pure, unadulterated ego. He wasn't just an escort to her anymore; he was a force of nature. He looked down at the top of her head, his fingers still knotted in her hair, and felt a flicker of contempt mixed with an overwhelming need to finish the job. The polished Mrs. Alistair was gone, replaced by a "bitch on heat" of his own making, her sharp authority now nothing more than a desperate plea for his presence.

He leaned forward, his weight shifting as he prepared to deliver the final blow to her dignity. He could see the conflict still warring behind her eyes—the ghosts of her family flickering in her gaze—and it only made him want to drive himself deeper. He wanted to reach those memories and overwrite them. He wanted every future thought she had of "home" or "duty" to be forever tainted by the memory of this floor-to-ceiling glass, the indifferent Detroit skyline, and the way she had begged for his touch.

As he eased the head of his shaft past her frantic, searching lips and toward the heat she had opened for him, Julius didn't feel a shred of guilt. He felt the heavy, rhythmic pulse of a man who had won. He wasn't just going to fuck her; he was going to colonize her, leaving her a hollowed-out shell of the woman she once was.

Julius began to ease himself forward, his thick girth stretching the entrance of her heat with a slow, relentless pressure. Mrs. Alistair closed her eyes as he edged in deeper, her breath catching in the back of her throat. Having tasted him only minutes before, she was already acutely aware that his anatomy was considerably thicker and longer than her husband's. She knew that even when he reached the depth her husband usually occupied, there would still be more of him to come. In that moment of complete surrender, she wanted all of it—every inch the benefactor had to offer.

He pushed forward again, forcing another two inches into her tightly stretched walls.

"Oh, fuck yes! More!" Mrs. Alistair begged, her voice a ragged shadow of its former self. The poised director had vanished; she was completely at ease now with the gutter talk he craved. "Push it all in! I want to feel your balls against me!"

"Feels good, does it, Mrs. Alistair?" he grunted, his muscles bunching as he forced his meat deeper still. "Is this the biggest you've ever taken?"

"Fuck, yes!" she cried, her head thrashing against the plush carpet.

"Bigger than your husband's?" Julius prompted, his voice a low growl, demanding the verbal confirmation of his victory over her past life.

"Oh, God! So much bigger!" she sobbed, the honesty of the betrayal stinging as much as the pleasure. "It feels like you're inside my womb... I've never been fucked so deep!"

"And hard," he added, beginning to saw his length in and out of her sopping core. His thick, veiny girth sent ripples of pleasure undulating outward, hitting the very edges of her consciousness. "Harder! Fuck me harder!" she screamed, her hands clawing at the muscles of his back. "Split me in two with it!"

Spurred on by the torrid words escaping her lips, Julius thrust violently forward. Mrs. Alistair automatically wrapped her legs around his waist, locking her ankles firmly at the small of his back. She pulled him deeper, welcoming the sensation of being nearly severed by his weight and power.

"Oh, shit!" she screeched uncontrollably. "It's so big... is my pussy tight enough for you?"

"It's the best," Julius gasped between heavy, lung-burning thrusts.

In her sexual frenzy, the compliment felt like the highest praise she had ever received. No gentle word from her husband had ever sparked a fire like this. Being told by this man—this escort—that she was his best lay was the only validation that mattered in the vacuum of the penthouse.

They rolled across the floor, locked in a desperate, sweating struggle for friction. The cold, hard surface of the floor tiles at the edge of the carpet scraped against Mrs. Alistair's bare skin, but she was beyond caring about the bruises. All she could think about was the rhythmic ramming of his shaft into her wet, aching center.

The orgasms began to build in waves. One minute he had her pinned, driving deep; the next, they rolled until she was on top, bouncing with a frantic energy on his thickness until she felt like she was floating in space. They rolled again, and she felt his weight return, his balls slapping against her as he drove home.

"Oh, you bastard! Play with my tits while you're screwing me," she pleaded desperately. "Suck on my nipples!"

As the words left her mouth, a sudden flash of her real life entered her mind—the office, her colleagues, the woman she was supposed to be. She imagined their shock and disgust if they could see her now, being used by the very man she was meant to be managing. But the truth was, she was out of control. If her husband would had walked in right then, she wouldn't have stopped; she would have demanded he finish her off anyway.

Julius leaned forward, yanking the cups of her bra down to release her breasts. Within seconds, his rasping tongue had her nipples standing rigid. She moaned in delight as he bit and sucked on each in turn, the sensation traveling like a live wire straight to her pussy. Then, she felt his hand slide down to where their bodies met. A finger began to tease back and forth over the sensitive, forbidden skin of her anus.

"Oh, God, no!" she cried out.

In all her years of marriage, she had never been touched there. The innocence of her past life recoiled, but the sensation was a revelation—arousing, terrifying, and utterly new. With his cock still buried deep inside her, he continued to toy with the entrance to her most private self, pushing her further into a world she no longer recognized.

The air in the suite was thick with the scent of sex and sweat, a stark contrast to the sterile, high-end luxury of the room. As Julius continued to toy with the entrance to her most private self, the physical sensation acted as a bridge between their two warring psyches.

Internally, Julius felt a cold, crystalline clarity. Every moan Mrs. Alistair uttered was a brick removed from the wall of her former life. To him, this wasn't just about the friction of her body; it was about the friction of her soul rubbing against the gutter. The finger he used to tease her was a flag planted on unconquered territory. He felt an almost God-like arrogance. He had taken a woman of high standing, a leader who moved in circles he usually only entered as a hired shadow, and reduced her to a chanting, desperate creature begging for more of his "filth." He watched her face—the way her eyes rolled back—and felt a surge of purely masculine ego. He was the one who had unlocked this; he was the one who had proven that her "respectability" was nothing more than a thin, silk veil, easily shredded.

For Mrs. Alistair, the internal experience was a terrifying split-screen. Half of her mind was screaming, a silent, high-pitched wail of grief for the woman she had been thirty minutes ago. She could see the faces of her family like fading photographs, their judgment a heavy weight. But the other half of her—the part currently being hammered into the floor—was experiencing a liberation so profound it was sickening. The shame didn't dampen the pleasure; it acted as an accelerant. Every time he touched her where her husband never dared, she felt a jagged thrill of "wrongness" that made her nerves sing. She was horrified to realize that she didn't want the "concerned mother" or the "foundation director" to come back. She wanted to stay in this dark, wet world where the only thing that mattered was the next thrust.

"Tell me," Julius rasped, his voice cutting through her internal fog like a blade. "Tell me who owns this pussy right now."

Mrs. Alistair's head thrashed against the carpet, her fingers digging into the hard muscles of his shoulders until she drew blood. The split in her mind finally snapped. The two halves of her existence fused into a single, white-hot point of Need.

"You!" she screamed, the word echoing off the floor-to-ceiling glass and out into the indifferent Detroit night. "You do! Julius... please! Finish it! Fuck me until I can't remember my own name!"

Spurred by her total capitulation, Julius's own control began to fray. He gripped her hips with bruising force, his thumbs digging into her hipbones as he began a final, brutal assault. The rhythm became frantic, a blurring of skin and sweat against the hard floor. He felt the tremors start deep within her—the rhythmic, desperate squeezing of her walls as she began to climax. The sensation triggered his own release, a tidal wave that crashed through him with enough force to make his vision blur. He buried himself one last time, pinning her to the floor with the full weight of his body as they both cried out into the empty, expensive air of the penthouse.

Mrs. Alistair tried to move, a final, flickering instinct of self-preservation urging her to push him off, terrified of where this new boundary might lead. But Julius was an immovable weight, his power absolute. Before she could find the strength to resist, he pushed a finger inside her most forbidden depth.

Her head tipped back, her mouth falling open in a scream that remained silent, trapped in her throat by the sheer intensity of the sensation. This wasn't just touch; it was an invasion. Each probe of his finger went deeper, reaming her out with a blunt force that brought forth pleasures she hadn't known the human body could contain. She was losing all control, her vision blurring at the edges as she teetered on the brink of blacking out.

"Oh, fuck yes! Fuck my ass, you pervert!" she cried, the words torn from her. She didn't just accept the sensation—she craved it. "Make me cum!"

She squeezed her eyes shut, the images of her husband, her colleagues, and her daughter flashing behind her eyelids like a series of car crashes. Even with these perverse thoughts flooding her mind, she knew she couldn't stop. Julius was an expert in her undoing; he knew exactly which buttons to press to maximize the thrill far beyond her wildest dreams.

The boss laid there, floundering like a fish out of water. The pleasure was too dense to navigate, too intense for her to even respond. With his mouth servicing her breasts, his dick deep in her pussy, and his finger plowing her anus, she felt as though she were orgasming in three places at once. In her lust-filled fugue, only one thing remained to make the humiliation complete: she wanted him to break with the same intensity she had.

"Oh God! Cum! Please cum!" she begged, her voice a broken whisper against the expensive carpet. "I want your hot cum filling my pussy!"

The words acted like a switch. She felt his anatomy grow that final, telltale inch—the same surge she had felt earlier when she'd taken him in her mouth. Her heart jumped into her throat in anticipation of the explosion. There was no finesse in his movements; Julius was a man driven by his own animal hunger, driving in and out of her as his finger continued its relentless pace.

The sound of his grunts should have disgusted her, yet they only served to heighten her arousal. She knew it was her doing—the fact that it was her body getting the powerful donor so worked up fueled her final descent. She could almost hear the muffled hiss of his release as he spurted deep inside her. He held her tight, his body locking rigid as his hot, sticky seed pumped into her. Within seconds, she felt the overflow leaking from her, spilling down her legs, yet he continued to pulse.

Realizing she could handle no more, she managed to guide him out from between her legs. Driven by a dark, newfound impulse, she had him kneel astride her. She watched as he spurted the remainder of his load over her heaving breasts. She had no idea how she had degenerated so far in a single morning, but the sight of his cream across her skin felt like a perverse badge of office. She reached up, smearing the warmth over her tits and massaging it into her nipples with a frantic, obsessive energy.

Julius knelt there for a moment, milking the last drops from his length until they dripped onto her skin. Then, he stood. Mrs. Alistair rose unsteadily for a moment before letting her weight sink down into the bed, her head finding the plush pillows as her designer jacket lay like a discarded skin on the floor. She watched him with a cold, calculating satisfaction, but as the silence stretched, her expression shifted. The boredom returned, and with it, a dangerous curiosity.

"You're very good, Julius," she said, her voice smooth and conversational now as he rested beside her. "Almost too good. It makes me wonder what else you're capable of."

She sat up, reaching for her handbag on the nightstand. She pulled out a small, translucent vial and a heavy, ornate silver lighter. She set them on the sheets between them.

"The protocol says no substances," Julius said, his voice a low warning. He felt the cold weight of the earpiece Carla had given him. "Carla was very specific."

Mrs. Alistair laughed, a dry sound that didn't reach her eyes. "Carla works for Dominic. And Dominic works for donors like me. I don't care about his 'protocols.' I want to see how far you'll go to keep that little sister of yours in her house."

She leaned closer, her eyes locked onto his. "I have a friend. A few floors down. He's... unconventional. He likes to watch, and he likes to participate in ways that would make Cynthia's skin crawl. I want you to come with me. And I want you to leave that earpiece right here on the nightstand."

Julius felt a chill that had nothing to do with the air conditioning. This was the line. Carla's voice echoed in his memory: *If she asks for something outside the protocol, you call me. Do not let the brand suffer.*

"I can't do that, Mrs. Alistair," Julius whispered.

"Can't you?" She reached out, her fingers tracing the scar on his rib. "I know about the eviction notice, Julius. I know exactly how many dollars stand between your family and the street. My friend downstairs? He'll pay enough to clear that debt tonight. No contracts, no years of service. Just one hour of... extracurricular work."

She watched him, the vial glinting in the low light. "So, what will it be? The loyal dog who follows Carla's rules, or the man who actually saves his family?".

Julius felt the room growing smaller, the walls of the Presidential Suite closing in like the bars of a cage. The temptation Mrs. Alistair dangled—the chance to bypass years of servitude and wipe Jazmine's debt clean in a single hour—was a siren song, but the memory of Dominic's bloody handkerchief and Carla's icy warnings acted as an anchor.

He knew these people. They didn't offer shortcuts; they only offered different ways to drown.

"I have my orders," Julius said, his voice flat and devoid of the heat that had filled the room moments before.

Mrs. Alistair's face contorted, the refined mask of the high-level donor slipping to reveal a spoiled, volatile child. "You're a fool, Sterling. You're choosing a leash over a lifeline."

Julius didn't answer. He reached up, his fingers brushing the cool plastic of the earpiece tucked behind his ear. He felt the weight of the moment—the choice to remain a "product" or risk becoming a casualty. He pressed the small button twice, the silent signal they had established if he couldn't speak freely.

Almost instantly, a faint, rhythmic static crackled in his ear. Carla was there. She was always there.

"Status," Carla's voice came through, a ghost in his head, cold and clinical.

Julius kept his eyes locked on Mrs. Alistair, who was now staring at him with a mixture of hatred and growing unease. She realized what he was doing. She reached for the vial on the bed, her movements frantic.

"Mrs. Alistair is requesting a deviation," Julius said aloud, his voice steady for the benefit of the microphone. "She's requested I disconnect and join her and her friend for some …extracurricular work. Whatever the fuck that means."

There was a pause on the other end. Then, Carla spoke, her tone sharpening into something lethal. "Do not move. Do not disconnect. Keep her in the suite. I am coming up."

"You're making a big mistake!" Mrs. Alistair hissed, lunging forward to grab the earpiece from his head.

Julius caught her wrists with a strength that was sudden and absolute. He didn't hurt her, but he held her in place, the "beast" now serving as a guard dog rather than a lover. The emerald silk bunched in his grip as he forced her to sit back on the edge of the bed.

"I was bought to protect the brand, Mrs. Alistair," Julius whispered, his face inches from hers. "And right now, you're the biggest threat to the investment."

The double mahogany doors of the suite burst open less than a minute later. Carla stepped in, followed by two men in dark suits who moved with the silent, heavy efficiency of professional shadows. Carla didn't look at the disheveled bed or the emerald silk on the floor. She walked straight to the nightstand, picked up the vial, and tucked it into her pocket without a word.

"Mrs. Alistair," Carla said, her voice like a sheet of ice cracking. "The car is waiting downstairs to take you home. Your 'friend' has already been... discouraged. Dominic will be in touch regarding your future contributions to the foundation."

Mrs. Alistair turned pale, her bravado evaporating instantly. She grabbed her handbag and fled the room without looking back, the two guards trailing her like reapers.

Silence reclaimed the suite. Julius stood by the window, his chest heaving, feeling the cold air of the hotel's climate control against his sweat-dampened skin. Carla walked over to him, her eyes scanning the marks on his shoulders.

"You did well, Julius," she said, her voice softening just a fraction—the first sign of humanity he'd seen from her. "You stayed on the path. Most men have taken the money, contaminate their bodies with that damn suga booger."

"The money wouldn't have kept us safe," Julius replied, his voice raspy.

"No," Carla agreed. She reached into her inner jacket pocket and pulled out a clean, white envelope. "But this might help. Consider it a bonus for your... discretion."

She handed him the envelope. Julius opened it to find ten thousand dollars in crisp hundreds. It wasn't enough to pay off the whole world, but it was enough to stop the orange notice in his pocket from becoming a reality.

“Go to the dressing room. Clean yourself up,” Carla commanded. “We have a breakfast meeting with the Cynthia in a couple hours.”

11

The transition from the sterile luxury of the Wellington to the morning air of Detroit was jarring. Julius felt the ten thousand dollars in the envelope against his thigh—a thick, heavy reminder of the night's transgressions and his narrow escape from Mrs. Alistair's trap.

The breakfast meeting took place at a secluded outdoor café on Bagley St. in Corktown, tucked behind a screen of ivy and wrought iron. The morning air was crisp, smelling of roasted coffee and diesel exhaust. Cynthia sat under a green umbrella, looking radiant in a sharp, cream-colored blazer. She didn't look like a woman who had spent the last forty-eight hours dismantling a man's soul; she looked like a leader ready to conquer the day.

"Carla told me about your performance last night," Cynthia said, as a waiter set a plate of poached eggs and avocado in front of her. She didn't offer Julius a seat at first, letting him stand in his tailored suit like a sentinel. "You showed remarkable restraint. Mrs. Alistair can be... persuasive."

"She was a risk to the pact and for that action, she was dismissed from the inner circle," Julius replied, his voice a low, disciplined rasp.

Cynthia smiled, a genuine expression of pride that made Julius's skin crawl. "Exactly. You're learning. You realized that the short-term gain she offered was a death sentence. Dominic is pleased also. And when Dominic is pleased, the world stays quiet."

She gestured for him to sit. "Eat quickly. I have a press conference at City Hall at eleven. You'll be driving the lead car. But before that..." she checked her watch, "you have about three hours. Go see your sister. Give her the 'bonus.' Make sure she understands that your new job is demanding, but rewarding."

The Lexus LS felt like an intruder as it rolled back onto the cracked asphalt of Main Street. The neighbors watched from behind frayed curtains as the gleaming black beast came to a silent halt in front of the duplex. Julius stepped out, the morning sun highlighting the sharp lines of his new suit. He didn't look like the brother who had left twenty-four hours ago. He looked like the men who owned the city. Jazmine was on the porch, holding Leo. Her face was weary, the dark circles under her eyes telling the story of another sleepless night. When she saw him, her hand tightened on the railing.

"Julius?" she whispered, her eyes roaming over the expensive fabric of his clothes. "You look... different."

"I told you the account was big, Jazz," he said, stepping up the creaking wooden stairs. The smell of the neighborhood—damp earth and old wood—hit him, grounding him for a fleeting second.

He reached into his pocket and pulled out the white envelope Carla had given him. He didn't say a word as he handed it to her. Jazmine opened it, her breath hitching as she saw the stacks of hundred-dollar bills.

"My god, Julius... where did this come from? This is more than you made in six months at the warehouse."

"It's a signing bonus. And hazard pay," he added, the truth hidden in the jargon. He reached into his other pocket and pulled out the crumpled orange eviction notice he had stolen from her table. He smoothed it out and handed it back to her. "I saw this yesterday. Pay it today. Pay the next three months in advance. Don't worry about the house anymore, Jazz. It's handled."

Jazmine started to cry, a mixture of relief and profound terror. "What are you doing, Julius? People don't just give out this kind of money. Not to people like us."

Julius leaned in, kissing her forehead and then ruffling Leo's hair. He felt the cold earpiece still in his pocket, a tether back to the monsters in Palmer Woods.

"I'm doing exactly what I have to do to keep you safe," he said, his voice firm. "I promised I'd see you, and I'm here. But the job is 24/7 now. I won't be around much, but the money will keep coming. Just... take care of you and Leo. Don't ask any more questions."

As Julius stepped inside the duplex, the familiar scent of cinnamon toast and floor wax hit him, a stark contrast to the sterile, expensive aroma of the Wellington. Jazmine followed him into his small bedroom; the envelope of cash clutched tightly against her chest.

Julius began to shed the midnight-black suit, his movements weary. He needed to change into one of the more "general" tailored outfits for the press conference—something that looked professional but stayed in the background.

"Julius, something happened at the clinic yesterday," Jazmine said, her voice trembling with a different kind of energy. "My supervisor... she called me into her office. They've been watching my numbers, my patient rapport. They offered me a promotion. Head of Patient Coordination."

Julius stopped unbuttoning his shirt, looking at her through the mirror. "That's amazing, Jazz. You've worked your ass off for that position."

"It's a massive raise," she continued, her words tumbling out. "Full benefits, a retirement plan, private schooling vouchers for Leo. But..." She paused, her eyes dropping to the floor. "It's at their facility. In Chicago."

The air in the room seemed to vanish. Julius turned around, his bare chest revealing the fading map of scratches and bruises—the physical toll of the life that was currently paying for her safety. He reached for a clean, charcoal-colored polo.

"Did you accept it?" he asked, his voice low.

"I told them I had to think about it. I didn't want to say "Yes" right then and there. Changing states, relocating Leo, leaving you. Didn't know if we could... if you'd want us to leave Detroit," she said.

Julius studied her. He saw the way she was standing—shoulders back, a flicker of hope in her eyes that he hadn't seen since the accident. Her body language spoke volumes; she was already imagining a life where she didn't have to look at orange eviction notices or hear sirens every night. She had already made her mind up.

"Jazz," he said softly, walking over to her. He took her hands in his. "Look at me."

She met his gaze, her eyes shimmering with unshed tears. "I love you. And I love Leo more than anything," Julius said, his voice thick with a sudden, sharp grief. He realized that if she moved to Chicago, he would be truly alone in the jaws of the pact. But he also realized it was the only way she would ever be truly safe from the people who owned him. "This is a big opportunity. A fresh start. You should take it."

"But what about you? This new job of yours..."

"My job is here," Julius interrupted gently, the lie settling into place like a tombstone. "I'm under contract, Jazz. Big firms don't let you just walk away. But knowing you and

Leo are in a good neighborhood, in a different city... it would make all of this worth it."

Jazmine let out a sob of relief, burying her face in his shoulder. Julius held her, his eyes fixed on the closet where the duffel bag was hidden. He was the anchor keeping her in the storm, and by cutting the rope, he was letting her drift toward the sun.

"Go to Chicago," he whispered into her hair. "Build that life for you and Leo. I'll come visit whenever I get some vacation time. I promise."

He pulled back, masking his heartbreak with a disciplined smile. "Listen to me," he interrupted, his voice steady but layered with an urgency he couldn't quite hide. "Go down to the rental office today. Pay every cent of the outstanding balance on this place. I don't want you leaving this city with a debt over your head or a mark on your name. Clear it all. Whatever is left over? That's your relocation fund. Use it for the movers, a deposit for Chicago, and whatever Leo needs for a new bedroom."

Jazmine bit her lip, looking at the money as if it might vanish. "This is a lot of money, Julius. Are you sure you're going to be okay? What if this firm... what if they want it back?"

"They won't," Julius said, the memory of Mrs. Alistair's predatory gaze flashing through his mind. The money was a drop in the bucket for them—a tiny price to pay for his absolute silence and service. "It's part of the deal. I'm doing this so you and Leo can have a clean break. No more orange notices. No more looking over your shoulder."

He saw the tension leave her shoulders, her body language shifting from defensive to a quiet, hopeful resolve. She was already mentally packing boxes, imagining a life where her brother didn't look like he had been dragged through hell. "I'll start looking at apartments tonight," she whispered, a small, genuine smile finally breaking through her worry. "Thank you, Julius. Truly."

"Don't thank me," he said, giving her a quick, tight hug that felt like a goodbye. "Just get him out of here, Jazz. Get him somewhere where the air is a little clearer."

He grabbed his keys and the new smartphone Cynthia had given him. As he walked out the door and toward the gleaming, armored Lexus, he felt a strange sense of peace. He was sinking deeper into the mud of the pact, but he had finally managed to push Jazmine and Leo onto dry land.

He climbed into the driver's seat, the leather cooling his skin. He had about an hour to get to the City Hall press conference. He adjusted his rearview mirror, catching a glimpse of the duplex before shifting into gear. He was a man with nothing left to lose now, which made him exactly what Dominic and Cynthia needed him to be. He had saved the house, but he knew he had lost his home.

The steps of Detroit City Hall were a hive of frantic energy. News vans with telescopic masts crowded the curb, and the air hummed with the collective murmur of reporters and city officials. Julius pulled the Lexus LS into the reserved lane, the car's dark windows reflecting the grand, neoclassical columns of the building like a mirror.

He stepped out, moving with a practiced, robotic grace. He opened the rear door for Cynthia, offering his hand. She emerged into a barrage of camera flashes, her cream blazer luminous in the morning light. She didn't just walk; she glided, a leader at the height of her powers, her smile fixed in a perfect, media-ready beam.

As they moved toward the podium, Julius fell back into his role, standing at a sharp diagonal behind her. He wore sunglasses despite the shadows of the building, his eyes scanning the crowd with a predator's focus. To the public, he was the new analyst for the city working under a rising star. To Cynthia, he was the ghost she had bought.

"The revitalization of our neighborhoods is not just a policy—it is a promise," Cynthia's voice rang out, clear and resonant, amplified by the microphones.

While the cameras were fixed on Cynthia, Carla appeared at Julius's side. She stood so close their shoulders nearly brushed, yet she didn't look at him. She stared straight ahead at the press corps, her face a mask of stone.

"Your sister seemed quite excited this morning," Carla said, her voice a low vibration that barely carried over the clicking of camera shutters. "The Patient Coordinator position in Downtown Chicago is a significant step up. It's a fine city for a childlike Leo."

Julius felt a cold jolt of electricity shoot down his spine. His hands tightened behind his back, but he didn't move a muscle. *How did she know?* He hadn't told anyone. Jazmine had only told him an hour ago.

Before he could process the invasion of his privacy, Cynthia finished a round of applause and stepped back, letting a city councilman take the mic. She leaned toward Julius, pretending to check a schedule, her perfume cloying in the heat.

"I hear the move to Chicago is officially happening, Julius," she murmured, her eyes dancing with a terrifying, knowing light. "It's a wonderful opportunity for Jazmine. I assume you've already discussed the logistics of the relocation?"

Julius felt the breath leave his lungs. "How did you know about the promotion?" Julius asked, his voice a jagged whisper, his eyes still fixed on the crowd to maintain the facade.

Cynthia's smile didn't falter. She looked back at the cameras, waving at a reporter she recognized. "We take an interest in the well-being of our associates' families, Julius. We find that people perform better when their loved ones are in the best situation possible"

The realization hit him like a physical blow. The promotion hadn't been a coincidence. The supervisor's sudden interest in Jazmine, the lucrative offer in a city five hours away—it was all part of the pact. They weren't just saving his sister; they were isolating him. They were moving his only vulnerability out of his reach and into their territory, ensuring that Julius would have no reason to look back, and no one to run to.

"She's happy," Julius managed to say, his heart heavy as lead. "That's all that matters."

"Exactly," Carla added from his other side, her voice a final, chilling note. "And as long as she stays happy in Chicago, you'll stay focused here. The system works, Julius. Don't fight it."

Cynthia stepped back to the podium for the closing remarks, her voice projecting hope and progress to the city of Detroit, while Julius stood behind her, a prisoner in a thousand-dollar suit, realizing that his sister's freedom was just another cage they had built for him.

The applause for Cynthia's closing remarks was deafening, a wall of sound that masked the quiet, lethal conversation happening behind the podium. As the reporters began to swarm for follow-up questions, Julius leaned slightly toward Carla, his gaze remaining fixed on the perimeter.

"Where's Dominic?" Julius asked, the question gnawing at him since he'd stepped onto the City Hall tiles. "I expected him to be here for something this high-profile."

Carla didn't look at him. She adjusted the cuff of her shirt, her movements stiff. "He's in the hospital, Julius."

Julius felt a flicker of surprise. He remembered the bloody handkerchief in the Tudor house, the ragged cough that had seemed to shake the very foundations of the porch. "Is it serious?"

"Dom is a private man," Carla said, her voice dropping to a somber, uncharacteristic hush. "He has a big heart—sometimes for his own good, and other times it's a liability. He's been fighting cancer for the last two years. He tried to keep it from Cynthia and I, thought he could shoulder the weight of a terminal diagnosis while still running this city from the shadows. We've known for a couple of months, but we didn't know how aggressive it truly was."

She finally turned her head, her eyes meeting Julius's for a split second. "He's a man who hates to appear weak. In his world, weakness is an invitation for wolves."

At that moment, Cynthia stepped back from the microphones, her professional smile still etched onto her face, but her hand was trembling as she reached for her phone. She looked at the screen, and the color drained from her cheeks. The polished, untouchable director suddenly looked small against the backdrop of the massive stone columns.

She had just received a call from the hospital.

"Carla," Cynthia whispered, her voice cracking. "They need us down at the hospital at once. They said... they said it isn't looking good."

The air around the three of them shifted. The triumph of the press conference vanished, replaced by the cold reality of mortality. Even with all the money, the armored cars, and the power to rewrite the lives of strangers, they couldn't rewrite the cell structure of the man at the top.

"Julius, the car," Carla commanded, her voice regaining its sharp edge. "Now."

Julius moved instantly. He cut a path through the lingering reporters, his shoulder-width frame acting as a snowplow for Cynthia as she hurried toward the curb. He threw open the door of the Lexus, and as they piled in, the silence of the armored cabin felt like a tomb.

He pulled away from City Hall, the tires screaming against the asphalt. In the rearview mirror, he saw Cynthia staring out the window, her hand clutching her phone as if it were a rosary. For the first time, Julius saw the cracks in the facade—the fear that if Dominic fell, the entire world they had built on secrets and blood might just come crashing down with him.

"Drive faster, Julius," Cynthia urged, her voice barely a breath. "Just get us there."

The hospital did not smell like the beeswax and aged mahogany of the Palmer Woods estate. Instead, it smelled of ozone, harsh bleach, and the metallic tang of impending finality. As Julius steered the Lexus through the emergency bay and followed Cynthia and Carla into the private wing, the transition was jarring. Here, the power they wielded over the city of Detroit meant nothing; the machines kept the rhythm now, not the pact.

In the sterile, fluorescent-lit waiting area of the ICU, Julius witnessed something he never expected to see: the vulnerability of his handlers. Cynthia, usually a portrait of unshakeable poise, was pacing the linoleum in her cream blazer, her polished heels making a frantic, hollow clicking sound. Her hair, perfectly coiffed for the cameras an hour ago, had begun to fray at the temples. She looked less like the "Head Bitch in Charge" and more like a terrified girl watching her world tilt on its axis.

Carla stood by the window, her back turned to the room. Her shoulders were rigid, but Julius saw the way her hands were balled into fists at her sides, shaking with a suppressed, silent rage against the one enemy she couldn't intimidate or outmaneuver.

"Mr. Sterling," a nurse whispered, approaching from the heavy double doors. "He's asking for Mr. Sterling."

Cynthia stopped pacing. She looked at Julius, her eyes wide and bloodshot. The fact that Dominic wanted the "product"—the man he had known for less than forty-eight hours—instead of his closest confidantes was a slap that left her speechless.

The heart monitor's steady pulse was the only thing grounding the room as Julius leaned over the bed. Dominic looked up, his eyes glassy but filled with an unexpected, lucid warmth. He didn't look like a kingpin anymore; he looked like a man settling his accounts with the universe.

The two weeks that followed Dominic's stay in the hospital were a blur of motion, a frantic dance between the dying past and a cold, demanding future. Julius lived his life in the gaps between heartbeats; his internal clock synchronized with the erratic rhythm of Dominic's monitor and the ticking of the moving clock in the duplex.

Every morning began in the gray light of dawn, helping Jazmine pack. The duplex was a maze of cardboard boxes and packing tape. Julius moved with a silent, mechanical efficiency, wrapping Leo's toys in bubble wrap and taping shut the boxes of Jazmine's nursing textbooks. He watched her through the haze of his own fatigue, seeing her excitement grow as his own world narrowed. He was building her a bridge to Chicago while his own feet were sinking into the Detroit mud.

By midday, the "beast" had to be dressed in Italian wool. Under Carla's tight direction, Julius spent his afternoons pleasing some of Dominic's legacy clients. These were the women who had funded the foundation for years—wealthy, lonely, or bored socialites who expected a certain level of... extracurricular attention or "and one" to an event. Julius performed his role with a hollow, polished grace. He was a phantom in their high-rise condos and suburban estates, giving them exactly what they wanted while his mind was already miles away, back in a hospital room that smelled of antiseptic and ozone.

Every evening, without fail, he returned to the hospital. He sat by Dominic's bed for hours, often in total silence. The nurses began to recognize him—the tall man in the expensive suit who arrived at 6:00 PM and didn't leave until little after eight or nine at night when he's scheduled. The tall man in the expensive suit who arrived at 6:00 PM until the early hours of the morning on his off days. Julius would read the news to him, or sometimes just sit and watch the city lights through the window, his hand resting near Dominic's skeletal one.

One night, as the rain hammered against the hospital glass, Carla found him slumped in the chair by Dominic's bed, his head back and eyes closed for a rare second of peace. She didn't wake him immediately. She stood in the doorway, watching the man who was burning himself at both ends to keep everyone else warm. When he finally jolted awake, his hand instinctively reaching for the earpiece he wasn't wearing, Carla stepped into the light.

Julius didn't look up when Carla approached. His gaze was fixed on the man in the bed, but his mind was miles and years away.

"He has the same look," Julius said, his voice a rough sandpaper rasp. "The determination. That way of pulling his curtains shut so no one can see what's burning inside. My father was exactly like that. Total privacy, right up until the end."

Carla moved closer, sensing the shift in the air. Julius let out a jagged breath.

"When the doctors told us about the cancer, they gave him three to five months. We pushed his life span close to three years. During that time, the privacy wall crumbled and I really known the man I called dad for so long, father and son unconditional love. And then, just like that, the clock was out of batteries."

He finally looked at her, his eyes bloodshot and gleaming with a sudden, frantic intensity.

"In the last years of his life, I decided then that I would be a vessel for him. I thought if I worked hard enough, stayed strong enough, he could just... live through me. Like I could carry his weight because his own legs couldn't do it anymore." He looked back at Dominic, the grief of those final moments with his father flooding back into the room like a rising tide. "Seeing Dominic like this... it's all coming back. Every bit of it."

Carla reached out, placing a steady hand on his shoulder. "I'll keep him company, Julius. I'm not leaving his side." She leaned in, her voice uncharacteristically soft. **"You're running on fumes, Julius."**

"The work isn't done," Julius replied, his voice cracking. He looked at Dominic, whose breathing had become a shallow, rhythmic rattle.

Julius stood up, his joints popping, the "beast" inside him too tired to even snarl. He leaned over and whispered a "see you later" to the unconscious Dominic, then walked out into the cold, wet night, a ghost-in-waiting for a life that was about to change forever.

12

By the end of the second week, the exhaustion had become a physical weight. His eyes were perpetually bloodshot, his ribs ached, and his voice had dropped to a permanent, raspy low. He was a man stretched across three lives—the brother, the asset, and the heir.

"I wasn't always the man in the Tudor house, Julius," Dominic rasped, a faint, nostalgic smile ghosting over his cracked lips. "Years ago, I was just a ghost in the night. A gigolo I was called. I sold my time, my body, and my discretion to the highest bidder. It was a hollow life until I met a young woman name Cynthia."

He paused, a wet cough rattling his chest. "She was fire. She was ambition. I left that world for her, but the world didn't leave me. She was beginning her professional career and I became a relationship consultant—architects for the youth who wanted to find what I had found: Love. We never said 'I do' in a church, Julius. We didn't need a piece of paper to validate a love that was stronger than the city itself."

Dominic's eyes drifted toward the door, where Carla's silhouette was visible through the frosted glass. "Carla came later. We found her in a place no child should ever know—surrounded by the rot of drug-addicted parents and a house that smelled of despair. We plucked her from that filth and made her ours. We gave her a world."

He turned his gaze back to Julius, his grip on the younger man's arm surprisingly firm. "I know about Jazmine and Leo. I know they are your world, just as Cynthia and Carla are mine. That's why I pulled some strings in Chicago. I wanted Jazmine to have the peace of mind to be the mother she is. I wanted her happy, so you could be focused."

Dominic took a shallow, hitching breath. "Cynthia... she's a brilliant judge of power, but a poor judge of character. She would never advocate for someone with bad intentions, which is why I've come to trust you so quickly. She saw something in you, maybe it was that beast!"

He leaned in closer, his voice a mere thread of sound. "I need you to look after them. My loves. Cynthia and Carla. They are sharp, but the world is sharper. The actual ledgers of past and present clients—the real ones—are hidden in the library, behind the casing of the third fireplace. Look for a slight indentation behind one of the stones. Go there. Take them. Give them to Cynthia when the time is right. The code is set to your birthday, Julius. I wanted it to be something you'd never forget."

Just then, Julius's phone buzzed in his pocket. He didn't need to look at it; he knew it was the reminder for his therapy appointment in 40 minutes—the last tether to his old, broken life. Dominic seemed to know it too. He knew this was the final curtain. With a monumental effort, he reached out his frail, trembling hand, palm open. Julius took it, the skin feeling like dry parchment. It wasn't the handshake of a master and a servant, but of two men who understood the cost of protection.

"See you later, Dominic," Julius whispered, the traditional farewell of those who don't believe in final goodbyes.

"See you later, son," Dominic replied, his eyes finally fluttering shut.

Julius stood up, his suit feeling ten sizes too small, the weight of the secrets and the dying man's trust pressing down on his shoulders. He walked out of the ICU room, his face a mask of iron. Cynthia and Carla were standing there, their faces etched with a raw, frantic hope.

Cynthia didn't wait. She moved past him in a blur of desperation. As Carla started to follow, Julius placed a gentle hand on her forearm, stopping her for a brief second.

"Carla," he said, his voice steady. "I have an appointment I have to get to. I'll be back as soon as I can."

Carla looked at him, her eyes searching his for any sign of finale in that room. She saw the gravity there. Slowly, she reached up and placed a hand on his shoulder, a rare gesture of solidarity. She nodded once, a silent acknowledgment of the weight he was now carrying, then turned and followed Cynthia into the room to say her own goodbye.

The drive to the therapist's office was the quietest thirty minutes of Julius's life. The Lexus moved through the midday traffic like a phantom, its cabin a soundproof vault that kept the world at bay. He looked at his hands on the leather-wrapped steering wheel—clean, manicured, and steady—and struggled to remember the man who had walked into this same clinic a month ago, shattered by the accident and drowning in a sea of guilt-driven compulsions.

He parked on a side street, the luxury car looking like a diamond in a coal bin. He stepped out, adjusted his charcoal blazer, and walked into the nondescript brick building. Dr. Alvarez looked up from her notepad as he entered. She had seen him at his worst, but today, she sat back, her eyes narrowing as she took in the expensive suit, the predatory grace of his posture, and the heavy, ancient stillness in his gaze.

"You look like a man who has finally found his cage, Julius," she said softly.

"I didn't come to talk about the cage, Doctor," Julius replied, sitting across from her. He felt the weight of the phone in his pocket, the one that linked him to a dying king and a brewing war. "I came to tell you that this will be our last session. The work is finished."

"And the hypersexuality? The impulsiveness you felt was a symptom of your trauma?"

Julius looked out the window, a small, sad smile playing on his lips. "It's not a symptom anymore. It's a tool. I've stopped fighting the 'beast' that we spoke of. I've accepted that part of me because it's the only part that can survive the world I just stepped into. The shame is gone, replaced by a utility I never asked for, but now deeply understand."

Dr. Alvarez watched him, a flicker of professional mourning in her eyes. She knew she was losing him to the shadows. "You're closing the door, then."

"I'm locking it," Julius said. He stood up, the movement fluid and decisive. "Thank you for trying to save the man I used to be. But he wouldn't have survived the month I just had."

He walked out without looking back, the bell on the clinic door chiming a final, lonely note. The Palmer Woods mansion felt hollow when he returned. The staff had been dismissed or were tucked away in the shadows, leaving the Tudor house to breathe its own history. Julius headed straight for the library—a room paneled in dark wood, rich with the smell of old leather and wealth. The smell of old paper and beeswax was heavy, the air stilled by the absence of its master.

He approached the third fireplace; a massive limestone structure carved with intricate vines. He ran his fingers along the side casing until he felt the slight indentation Dominic had described. He pressed it, and with a soft, mechanical hiss, a hidden panel swung inward.

Inside sat a heavy, leather-bound ledger—the true heart of the pact. He pulled it out, his fingers trembling slightly.

He turned the brass dial of the small internal safe, entering the numbers of his own birthday. *Click.* The lock gave way. As he pulled the book into the light, his phone vibrated in his palm. It was Carla. He didn't even have to answer to know what she was going to say.

"He's gone, Julius," she whispered, her voice a jagged shard of glass. "Dominic is gone."

Julius didn't hang up, but he stopped listening. He stood before the massive, arched picture window of the library. Outside, the world was playing a cruel trick of nature. The sky was a brilliant, piercing blue—not a single cloud marred the horizon. Yet, despite the clear sky, a sudden, torrential rain began to fall.

The sun caught the raindrops as they streaked against the glass, turning them into falling diamonds. The room was flooded with a golden, ethereal light even as the storm hammered against the panes. It was a "sun shower," a beautiful, weeping contradiction.

Julius gripped the ledger against his chest, watching the golden rain. The man who had assist with his lifestyle change before has died, the sister he loved was leaving, and the life he had once known was buried under a pile of old coats in a duplex he could never truly call home again. He was the guardian of the secrets now, standing in the light of a sun that offered no warmth, drenched by a rain that came from a cloudless sky.

Days later, the burial of Dominic Preston has begun. The air at Woodlawn Cemetery was crisp, smelling of damp earth and expensive floral arrangements. Julius stood between Cynthia and Carla, his dark suit absorbing the pale afternoon light. The burial of Dominic Gallaway was over, the finality of the dirt hitting the casket still echoing in his mind.

"I'll be back," Julius said softly, his voice barely rising above the rustle of the wind. "I need a moment."

Cynthia reached out, her gloved hand grazing his arm. "Take your time, Julius. We aren't going anywhere."

He nodded, turning away from the fresh mound of Dominic's grave. He walked with a steady, purposeful gait toward the massive stone mausoleum nearby. The structure was a fortress of silence, a stark contrast to the whispered condolences of the crowd behind him.

Carla watched his retreating figure, her brow furrowing with a mix of confusion and concern. She wrapped her arms around herself, shivering as a sudden gust of wind whipped through the towering oaks.

"Where is he going?" Carla asked, her voice a fragile whisper. "The service is over. Why is he heading toward the mausoleums?"

Cynthia didn't turn her head. She kept her eyes fixed on Julius until he disappeared behind the heavy glass doors of the stone structure. A sad, knowing smile touched her lips, though her eyes remained glassy with unshed tears.

"A man can only carry so much grief before he has to share the weight," Cynthia said, her voice steady but heavy with emotion. She turned to Carla, tucking a loose strand of hair behind the younger woman's ear. "He isn't leaving us, Carla. He's just visiting the only people who knew him before he had to be this strong. He's going to see his lost loved ones."

Through the double glass doors, Julius made a sharp right. He stepped down a long hallway where the overhead lights flickered to life, section by section, triggered by his movement to save on electricity. The clinical hum of the lights followed him like a mechanical heartbeat. When he reached the end of the hallway, he stopped in front of a simple wooden bench. There, set into the wall, lay the bodies of **Wesley Sterling, Nessie Sterling, and Nathaniel Sterling**: his parents and his brother.

The sight of their names carved into the polished stone hit him like a physical weight. He approached the slab, his reflection ghosting over the letters. He reached into his inner coat pocket and pulled out three long-stemmed roses, their petals a deep, bruised crimson. Moving his fingers over their names, he felt the biting cold of the stone before carefully placing the roses into the flower holder. He eased himself onto the hard bench.

"In the name of the Father, the Son, and the Holy Spirit," he whispered, bowing his head and rekindling his catholic school days.

The conversation that followed was brief but powerful. He updated them on everything—the highs that would have made his family proud and the lows that would have nearly brought them to his knees.

"I'm sorry it took me so long to visit," he apologized, his voice cracking slightly in the empty hall. "I was trying to find a way to balance life... to figure out how to be who you need me to be while carrying all of this."

He said his goodbyes, the weight in his chest feeling slightly lighter as he stood to leave. As Julius exited the building, the driver of the limo pulled the car right to the doors. Julius slid into the back, the heavy door sealing out the cemetery air as they began the drive back to the Palmer Woods mansion.

Julius stood near the towering mahogany doors, nursing a glass of sparkling water. He felt like a sentry guarding a tomb. He watched the small, formal group of mourners disperse, each one exchanging hushed, calculated words with Cynthia and Carla. These were the power players of Detroit, men and women who dealt in favors and silence, all of them sizing up the two women to see if the empire would hold.

Then, the air in the room seemed to shift. Julius saw them. Jazmine and Leo entered the room. Jazmine walked with a resolute stiffness, her chin tucked but her eyes clear, holding Leo's hand so tightly her knuckles were white. They had come to pay their respects to the man who had inadvertently saved them, and to say a final goodbye to the brother she was leaving behind.

Jazmine walked straight to Cynthia, who was seated in the middle of a velvet sofa beside the massive marble fireplace. She looked weary, her dark eyes assessing Jazmine with a sharp, habitual scrutiny that softened almost instantly when they rested on Leo.

"Ms. Cynthia," Jazmine said, her voice respectful but firm. "This is my son, Leo."

Cynthia looked up, her expression settling into a tone of sorrowful elegance. "Thank you for coming," she replied.

"We wanted to offer our sincere condolences for your loss," Jazmine continued, her voice unwavering even in the face of such overwhelming wealth. "And to apologize for leaving so quickly. We have a long travel ahead of us to Chicago."

Cynthia gave a slow, knowing nod. "I understand completely, Jazmine. Family first."

The exchange was brief but effective. The jagged edges of their first meeting at the duplex—the suspicion, the fear—seemed to melt away in the shared gravity of the room. Cynthia stood, and for a moment, the two women shared a hug and a quiet cry, a bridge built over a river of secrets.

"You be safe, Jazmine," Cynthia said, pulling back and smoothing her black silk dress. "And when you get settled in Chicago, you absolutely must try Pizzeria Portofino. Their burrata is to die for." It was a cold, high-society recommendation, delivered with an unnerving sense of normalcy that only Cynthia could master.

"We will," Jazmine said with a small, sad smile. She turned her gaze to Julius, her eyes brimming. "Take care of brother for me."

Cynthia's eyes flickered toward Julius, a predatory glint returning to her gaze. "He will be in *good* hands."

Julius stepped forward, holding the keys to the duplex, to Jazmine's new CRV parked around the bend of the long, winding driveway. He walked up to the backdoor, opening the door for Jazmine to place Leo in his seat. His shadow stretching long and skeletal across the gravel. She rolled the glass down before closing the door, her eyes puffy and red-rimmed.

"Jaz," he said softly, his voice catching the evening chill. "I didn't just come from the house earlier. After the funeral, I went to see Mom, Dad, and Wesley."

The air between them grew still, the heavy scent of funeral lilies from the mansion replaced by the smell of damp earth and cooling pavement.

"You went to see them?" she whispered, her voice trembling.

"I did," Julius replied, his gaze drifting toward the horizon where the sun had finally dipped out of sight. "I walked down that long hallway—the one where the lights flicker on as you pass. It was so quiet in there, Jaz. Just me and them."

He reached into his mind, picturing the three roses he had tucked into the stone holder and the way the carved names of Wesley, Nessie, and Nathaniel had felt beneath his fingertips.

"I told them everything," he continued, his eyes meeting hers again. "I told them about the highs, the lows... and the mess we're trying to navigate now. I apologized for staying away so long. I told them I was just trying to find a way to balance it all without breaking."

A single tear escaped Jazmine's eye, trailing a path through her makeup. She reached out, squeezing Julius's hand—the one still clutching the keys to their old life.

"Did it help?" she asked, her voice barely audible over the low hum of the idling engine.

"Ya, it actually did. Also, it reminded me of the weight we carry," Julius said, his expression hardening into one of somber resolve. "And it reminded me why I have to keep going. I told them I'd look out for you and Leo. Always."

Jazmine nodded slowly, a look of profound relief washing over her tired features. "Thank you for going, Julius. I haven't been able to bring myself to step inside that building since the funeral. Knowing you were there... it makes the distance feel a little smaller."

"Go on," he said softly, leaning down to give Leo one last squeeze through the window. He stood on the driveway and watched the car pull away once more, the red taillights finally disappearing for good. He was alone now, standing in the shadow of Cynthia's new empire, clutching the keys to a house that was now just a shell of memories. He was the master of the duplex and the servant of the mansion, and as he turned back toward the house to face the "beast" of his new life, he slipped the keys deep into his pocket, where they sat cold and silent against his thigh.

Julius let out a long, shuddering breath, feeling the last thread of his old life snap. He walked back inside the house, a silent observer among the dwindling mourners. He found himself looking out at a tree in the yard, its leaves blossoming in the late spring air—a cruel reminder that life continued even when the world ended. Another chapter was beginning in a very short lifespan.

"Julius…"

Cynthia and Carla appeared from the archway of the back parlor. When he turned, Cynthia gave a sharp, silent indication to follow her. No more words were needed.

They entered the rear of the mansion, stepping into the dim, wood-paneled study. Julius and Carla took their individual leather chairs while Cynthia walked around the heavy oak desk that had once been Dominic's. She paused, her eyes locking onto a small leather booklet sitting in the center of the desk, overshadowing the folder for the next client.

She picked it up, her breath hitching as she flipped through the pages. She saw names she recognized—and many she didn't. These were the true ledgers. The hidden debts. The heart of the city's shadow.

"Who… was it you?" Cynthia questioned, her eyes burning as she looked at Julius.

"Dominic informed me of the location," Julius said, his voice now a steady, resonant baritone. "He told me to give it to you when the time was right. I feel that the time is right now to succeed. Confucius said, 'Success depends upon previous preparation, and without such preparation there is sure to be failure.'"

Cynthia looked at Carla, a slow, triumphant smile spreading across her face.

"You chose a good one, CeCe! He putting that Confucius voodoo shit on you!" Carla said, crossing her legs with a look of pure satisfaction.

Cynthia took a deep breath before sitting in Dominic's old leather chair. She was the head of the table now, the ruler of the secret life behind the success of Detroit. She shifted the ledger to the side and pulled the new client folder in front of her.

"Julius," Cynthia said, her voice dropping into a professional chill. "Close the door."

Julius stood. He felt a surge of confidence, the images of his past life—the accident, the therapy, the duplex—flashing before his eyes like a dying fire. He reached for the heavy brass handles of the pocket doors. With a firm, decisive *clack*, he slid them shut. The sound was the official end of Julius Sterling.

He turned and faced the silent, wealthy room, ready to begin his new life as Julius Steele, an asset for the city of Detroit and of Cynthia's empire. The journey had begun, and there was no turning back.

www.ingramcontent.com/pod-product-compliance
Lightning Source LLC
La Vergne TN
LVHW090601110826
845146LV00001B/219